How would the English village of St. Mary Mead have survived its crime wave without Agatha Christie's sleuth, Miss Jane Marple?

Anne Hart, Miss Marple's biographer, tells us that "a search through Marpelian literature will reveal that over a period of some forty years, there occurred in St. Mary Mead a total of sixteen murders — five by poisoning, two by shooting, two by drowning, two by strangling, and five by unidentified means — plus four attempts at murder by poisoning, smothering, and bashing on the head."

Moreover, in that same period there also "occurred five robberies, eight embezzlements, two series of blackmailing, several illegal impersonations, a case or two of poaching, and a number of crank phone calls, poison-pen letters, and criminal libels.

"Faced with these statistics, one cannot help but count St. Mary Mead fortunate in having had, in the same period of time, a resident sleuth of the stature of Miss Marple…"

THE LIFE AND TIMES OF
MISS
JANE MARPLE

BY ANNE HART

BERKLEY BOOKS, NEW YORK

Grateful acknowledgment is made to Harold Ober Associates, Inc.
and William Collins Sons & Co. Ltd. for permission to
quote from the works of Agatha Christie.

This Berkley book contains the complete
text of the original hardcover edition.

THE LIFE AND TIMES OF MISS JANE MARPLE

A Berkley Book / published by arrangement with
Dodd, Mead & Company, Inc.

PRINTING HISTORY
Dodd, Mead & Company edition published 1985
Berkley edition / April 1987

ISBN: 0-425-09708-0

A BERKLEY BOOK ® TM 757,375
Berkley Books are published by The Berkley Publishing Group,
200 Madison Avenue, New York, NY 10016.
The name "BERKLEY" and the stylized "B" with design
are trademarks belonging to Berkley Publishing Corporation.

PRINTED IN THE UNITED STATES OF AMERICA

For a very dear aunt,
Anita Elliott Baird,
whom Miss Marple would have
enjoyed knowing

Contents

Preface

It has been a great pleasure to write this biography of Agatha Christie's beloved and resilient Miss Marple, the best known of a notable group of women who have played leading roles in detective fiction. Of course, not a word of this book would have been written had not a benevolent genius created Miss Marple in the first place, and I am immensely grateful to Rosalind Hicks, Agatha Christie's daughter, for giving her kind approval for my use of her mother's writing in this way.

Unlike other biographers, I cannot claim to have unearthed new material. Everything we know of Miss Marple is contained in the twelve books and twenty short stories devoted to her remarkable sleuthing. To search through these books and stories, not for murderers but for clues to Miss Marple herself, is the aim of this biography. I hope its readers will enjoy reading it as much as I have enjoyed writing it. Together we are indebted to the incomparable Agatha Christie.

I am grateful to a number of people who have encouraged me along the way. I would particularly like to thank Susan Hart, Nancy Grenville, David Grenville, and Percy Janes for their helpful advice on the manuscript, and June Mescia, my editor at Dodd, Mead, for her suggestions and good judgment.

One

St. Mary Mead

For me, as for many others, the reading of detective stories is an addiction like tobacco or alcohol . . . the story must conform to certain formulas (I find it very difficult, for example, to read one that is not set in rural England).
     —W.H. Auden, "The Guilty Vicarage"

"Give me a nice cup of tea, Aunt Jane, with some thin bread and butter and soothe me with your earliest remembrances of St. Mary Mead."
     —Inspector Craddock, *The Mirror Crack'd*

The pretty village of St. Mary Mead will be forever known as the home of Miss Jane Marple, that wonderful sleuth whose creator so cleverly, and for so many years, led us down the garden path. It is impossible, indeed, to imagine St. Mary Mead without Miss Marple or Miss Marple without St. Mary Mead; it was the archetypal English village created just for her. That for almost fifty years its pleasant homes and byways were so frequently the scenes of crimes has never detracted in the least from its essential coziness and charm. Before fully introducing Miss Marple, it is first necessary to introduce St. Mary Mead.

St. Mary Mead lies in the home county of Downshire (occasionally called Radfordshire) and is about twenty-five miles south of London and twelve miles equidistant from Market Basing* and the coast at Loomouth. Danemouth, a fashionable watering place also on the coast, is about eighteen miles from the county town of Much Benham and it, in turn, is two miles from St. Mary Mead.**

Of its history and the origins of its name we know nothing. It is true that a well-known archaeologist once came down to St. Mary Mead to excavate an ancient barrow in the grounds of Old Hall, but the subsequent discovery that he was merely an impostor out to steal Colonel Protheroe's Georgian trencher salts and Charles the Second *tazza* appears to have ended a brief flurry of interest in village antiquities. A concern for local history

* A charming country town and a favorite haunt during the 1920s and 1930s of a well-known contemporary of Miss Marple's, M. Hercule Poirot. See *Poirot Loses a Client* and *The Market Basing Mystery*.

** At risk of further confusing the reader, it should be added that Miss Marple's St. Mary Mead is not the village of the same name described in *The Mystery of the Blue Train*. That St. Mary Mead is in Kent.

cannot be found listed as an activity in St. Mary Mead; day-to-day affairs and distractions seem to have left its inhabitants with little time to greet tourists or dwell on any but the most recent events.

An interesting map of St. Mary Mead is to be found in that useful early guide, *The Murder at the Vicarage*. A few additions—principally signposts to Gossington Hall and Much Benham, and an indication of the new Development—have been added to bring the geography of the village up to date. As can be seen from this map, St. Mary Mead is a small village whose shops and houses straggle comfortably along the High Street from the Railway Station at one end to the Blue Boar at the other. Three houses, including the Vicarage, face onto a side road, and in this area are several footpaths and lanes leading to and from the neighboring woods and fields. Old Hall, one of the two "big houses" of St. Mary Mead, can be approached by one of these. The other big house, Gossington Hall, lies about a mile and a quarter along the Lansham Road to the northeast. To reach it one passes a new building estate boasting a flourish of half-timbered, sham Tudor houses rejoicing in "distorted rustic" gates and names such as "Chatsworth." This new building estate, laid out in the late 1920s, should not be confused with the more plebeian Development, whose many houses and television masts sprang up in the early 1960s, obliterating the pleasant meadows where Farmer Giles's cows once used to graze.

Fortunately these newer areas are tucked well away from the High Street and out of view. If one drove through

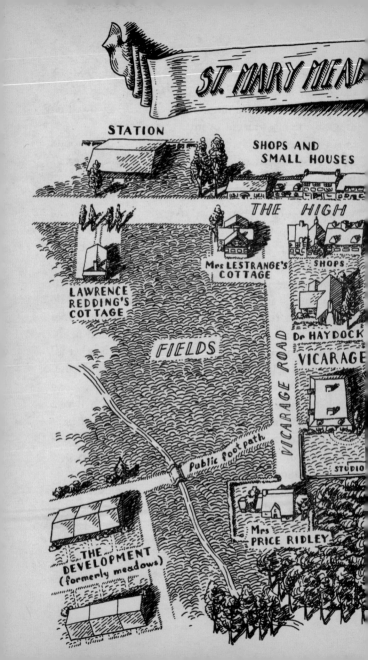

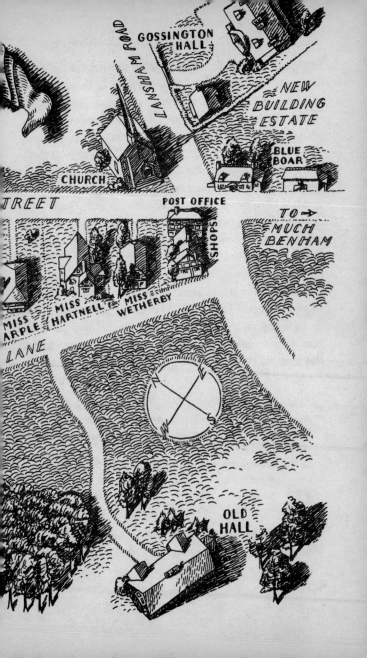

St. Mary Mead today, it would present much the same aspect as it did forty or fifty years ago. It is regrettable, of course, that the fishmonger has chosen to install an unsightly plate-glass window, and the gleaming new supermarket, which replaced the basket shop, remains anathema to the older generation ("All these great packets of breakfast cereal instead of cooking a child a proper breakfast of bacon and eggs"). Yet the old-world core, as Miss Marple liked to think of it, is still there—the church, the vicarage, and the "little nest of Queen Anne and Georgian houses" where lived, in the good old days, that formidable triumvirate of village spinsters, Miss Marple, Miss Hartnell, and Miss Wetherby.

It is pleasant to imagine oneself back in those days. Where to begin? Perhaps 1935 could be arbitrarily chosen as a good year. Any number of unusual things had happened there in the preceding ten years and, to add to the interest, everyone still knew (almost) everyone else. As Miss Marple was to put it fifteen years later:

> "They were people whose fathers and mothers and grandfathers and grandmothers, or whose aunts or uncles, had lived there before them. If somebody new came to live there, they brought letters of introduction, or they'd been in the same regiment or served in the same ship as someone there already. If anybody new—really new—really a stranger—came, well they stuck out—everybody wondered about them and didn't rest till they found out."

The people who never rested in such inquiries were Miss Marple, Miss Hartnell, and Miss Wetherby, the old guard of ladies in reduced circumstances who lived in neat houses round the church, and who knew intimately all the ramifications of the county families even though they might not be strictly county themselves.

Not everyone spoke of them so mildly: "old cats" . . . "old pussies" . . . "tea and scandal at four-thirty." Even Colonel Melchett, who was to become one of Miss Marple's greatest admirers, was heard to exclaim, "Too many women in this part of the world."

Miss Hartnell, who lived next door to Miss Marple, was described by the Vicar as "weather-beaten and jolly and much dreaded by the poor." Of Miss Wetherby, who lived next door to Miss Hartnell, he wrote that she "is a mixture of vinegar and gush." Earlier in the same paragraph he had described Miss Marple as "a white-haired old lady with a gentle, appealing manner" and went on to conclude, "Of the two Miss Marple is much the more dangerous." In one sense he was right. Miss Marple *was* dangerous, but not as a scandalmonger, as the Vicar had first supposed.

Fortunately for St. Mary Mead, Miss Marple emerged from the ranks of the ruling spinsters as a first-class detective, her wits and ingenuity well cultivated on the village grapevine. The mystery of Miss Wetherby's missing gill of shrimps, the case of Miss Hartnell's stolen opal pin, the affair of the Churchwarden's separate establishment all prepared Miss Marple well for the wave of murders, attempted murders, robberies, and embezzlements that were to engulf St. Mary Mead for the next forty years.

Apart from the censorious spinsters, did St. Mary Mead have a ruling class? In the normal scheme of village life, of course, it was really supposed to be the landed gentry, the old county families who lived in the big houses. But Downshire could not claim to be a fashionable hunting county, and in the St. Mary Mead of those prewar days the owners of Old Hall and Gossington Hall tended to be relative newcomers—comfortably off, to be sure, but with attitudes and conduct not noticeably distinguishable from those of the village's middle class.

At Gossington Hall, "Good, solidly built, rather ugly Victorian," lived the Bantrys, who were likable and unpretentious. Colonel Bantry, bluff, "red-faced, broad-shouldered," was the principal magistrate of the district, read *The Times*, and defended the Empire. His wife, Dolly, who became one of Miss Marple's closest friends, was a dear.

Old Hall was a big Victorian house surrounded by parkland and woods. These woods proved a particularly good place in which to set alibi-providing time fuses, bury incriminating evidence, and dig up rocks for Miss Marple's Japanese garden. The deserted North Lodge of Old Hall had its uses as well. It was an excellent place from which to make anonymous phone calls.

Old Hall will always be remembered as the home of the odious Colonel Protheroe of *The Murder at the Vicarage*. In his day the front door of Old Hall was opened by a butler, while in the wings hovered a housekeeper, a parlormaid, a cook, a kitchen maid, a valet, and a chauffeur. After Colonel Protheroe's sudden demise Old Hall fell on hard times. Put up for sale, it proved unlettable and unsalable until "an enterprising speculator had divided it into four flats with a central hot-water system, and the use of 'the grounds' to be held in common by the tenants."

At the crossroads, about midway between Old Hall and Gossington Hall, stood the parish church. "Our little church," the Vicar called it, and went on to add proudly that it had an interesting screen, "some rather fine old stained glass, and, indeed, the church itself is well worth looking at."

Occasionally a handful of the inhabitants, usually newcomers, appear to have dabbled in faiths other than that of the Church of England: to have toyed with spiritualism, for example, or the Oxford Group (like young Ted Gerard, who owned up to embezzlement), or Wesleyanism (whose minister refused to let his child get her teeth fixed because it was the Lord's Will if they stuck out). Generally speaking, however, most of the villagers were firmly, if not militantly, Church of England. As Miss Marple once put it, "in my own village, St. Mary Mead, things do rather revolve round the church"; and indeed its parishioners, particularly the women, appear to have supported an impressive round of activities. There was the Women's Institute, perpetually skirmishing with the District Nurse and the village schoolmistress, the W.V.S., and the Mothers' Union; there was the Needlework Guild and the Sales of Work; there were the Boy

Scouts, the Brownies, and the Girl Guides; there were the Choir Boys' outings and the Boys' Club cricket matches; there was the Society for the Propagation of the Gospel, the St. Giles Mission, and the Bishop's Appeal for the Deep-Sea Fishermen; there was the St. John Ambulance, the Nave Restoration Fund, and the Church of England Men's Society; there were committees to look after unmarried mothers, the workhouse, and the orphanage. The list goes on and on.

Collecting moral and financial support for all these worthy causes was an important social activity in itself. Appropriate small black book in hand, one could knock at any door, distributing gossip with the annual Armistice Day poppies and receiving back what often proved to be valuable pieces of information. Miss Marple found this a particularly helpful method of investigation in some of her more difficult cases. Of course, in collecting, as in so many aspects of life in St. Mary Mead, unfortunate episodes did occur. Not soon forgotten was "the woman who came down here and said she represented Welfare, and after taking subscriptions she was never heard of again," nor Mrs. Partridge, who appropriated to her own use seventy-five pounds of Red Cross donations.

Presiding, uneasily at times, over these various parochial activities was the Vicar of St. Mary Mead. Over the years a number of clerics occupied this post, the most memorable of whom was the Reverend Leonard Clement, one of the most likable men in Marpelian literature and, as the narrator of *The Murder at the Vicarage*, an author in his own right. While his irrepressible wife Griselda and his parishioners regarded him as hopelessly absent-minded and unworldly, "a gentle, middle-aged man [who] was always the last to hear anything," his writings reveal an unexpectedly astute grasp of village affairs. "At my time of life," he wrote, "one knows that the worst is usually true." One cannot help but suspect that much of this gentle Vicar's vagueness and detachment was a defense mechanism adopted against the vagaries of his flock. He had to endure the fluttering parish ladies who quarreled over the church decorations and gave him bedsocks for Christmas; an organist who was "very peculiar indeed" over young girls, succeeded by another who objected to the choirboys sucking sweets; a handsome young curate who proved embarrassingly attractive to the parish ladies, followed by another whose High Church "becking and nodding and crossing himself" enraged the parishioners almost as much as his embezzlement of their Sunday Evensong offertories; the unpopular churchwarden who was found shot in the head in the Vicar's own study. No one could say that St. Mary Mead was an easy incumbency.

In his personal life, the Vicar appears to have wrestled constantly with temptation: his desire to read the latest detective novel, for example, instead of preparing next Sunday's sermon; his continual longing for a decent meal; above all, his unseemly infatuation for his young wife, Griselda, who was indeed the antithesis of the traditional vicar's wife. She claimed to have chosen her middle-aged husband over a "cabinet minister, a baronet, a rich company promoter, three subalterns, and a n'er-do-well with attractive manners" and never to have regretted her decision: "It's so much nicer to be a secret and delightful sin to anybody than to be a feather in his cap." As a housekeeper she was a disaster. "Bad food and lots of dust and dead wasps is really nothing to make a fuss about," she once said, and, it must be admitted, none of these things seems to have deterred either the spinster brigade or the tennis-party set from making Griselda's untidy drawing room their rallying point.

Besides Miss Marple, the Clements had two other neighbors: Mrs. Price Ridley and Dr. Haydock. Mrs. Price Ridley was a "rich and dictatorial widow" whose immaculate house stood on the other side of the vicarage wall. Though not a spinster, she was an important member of the tea-and-scandal group and, to the Vicar's secret regret, a devout churchgoer. On the other side of the Clements lived Dr. Haydock, the physician and police surgeon. "Haydock is the best fellow I know," wrote the Vicar, and Colonel Melchett said of him, "He's a very sound fellow in police work. If he says a thing, it's so."

From time to time strange birds of passage alighted in St. Mary Mead, causing no end of a stir. Mention has been made of the bogus archaeologist who came to dig in the grounds of Old Hall. Other examples of this phenomenon were Mrs. Spenlow, a lady with a past, who was found on her hearthrug, strangled by a tape measure, shortly after coming to live in St. Mary Mead; Rex Stanford, an inoffensive young architect who was framed for a murder within a month of his arrival; and flamboyant Basil Blake, who came down to live in one of the sham

Tudor houses on the new building estate, bringing with him noisy weekend guests and a permanently resident platinum blonde.

Two other strangers who set the dovecotes fluttering, and whose cottages appear on the *Murder at the Vicarage* map, were Lawrence Redding and Mrs. Lestrange.

"He's a very good-looking young fellow," said Miss Wetherby of Lawrence Redding. "But loose," replied Miss Hartnell. "Bound to be. An artist! Paris! Models! The Altogether!" The Vicar kindly lent his garden shed as a studio to this young artist, and in it all Miss Hartnell's worst prophecies were realized. But no one, not even Miss Marple, could learn much about the appropriately named Mrs. Lestrange, and if her ex-husband had not died under mysterious circumstances, her secrets would probably have been safe to this day.

Little Gates, Mrs. Lestrange's house, had formerly belonged to a retired Anglo-Indian colonel, a far more familiar type of newcomer. Indeed, there were a number of collections of brass tables and Burmese idols scattered around St. Mary Mead: Major Vaughan at The Larches, for example, and Colonel Wright at Simla Lodge. *Bearers, tigers, chota hazri, safari,* and *Kikuyu* became familiar words. But these soldierly old boys and their wives were never regarded as strangers (i.e., primary criminal suspects). Armed with letters of introduction and an old regimental tie, the retired general or commander who came to live in St. Mary Mead was welcomed as "one of us."

Two other important people in St. Mary Mead were

the bank manager and the solicitor. In the early days the solicitor was Mr. Petherick, "a dried-up little man with eye-glasses which he looked over and not through." After his death, his son carried on the family business, but for some reason we learn little of him or of Mr. Wells, his successor, except that young Ronnie Wells left St. Mary Mead for East Africa to start a series of cargo boats on the lakes and lost all his money in the venture.

The St. Mary Mead branch of Middleton's bank stood at 132 High Street. "Do you remember Joan Croft, Bunch?" Miss Marple once asked a goddaughter. "Used to stalk about smoking a cigar or a pipe. We had a Bank hold-up once, and Joan Croft was in the Bank at the time. She knocked the man down and took his revolver away from him. She was congratulated on her courage by the Bench." Alas, this is all we ever learn of Joan Croft.

Over the years Miss Marple reminisced about several different bank managers and their families. There was Mr. Hodgson, who "went on a cruise and married a woman young enough to be his daughter. No idea of where she came from." There was Mr. Eade, "a very conservative man—but perhaps a little too fond of money." Young Thomas Eade, his son, turned out to be a bit of a black sheep and ended up in the West Indies. "He came home when his father died and inherited quite a lot of money. So nice for him." And there was Mr. Emmett, who had married beneath him with the unfortunate result that his wife "was in a position of great loneliness since she could not, of course, associate with the wives of the trades people."

Miss Marple no doubt produced this particular "of course" with her head "a little on one side looking like an amiable cockatoo," for there it was, the undeniable fact that St. Mary Mead was divided into two worlds, with an overall consensus that things went much more comfortably if everyone stuck to the one in which the Good Lord had caused them to be born. Which brings us to that section of the village map marked "Shops and Small Houses" and the people who lived and worked in them.

The fishmonger's, which stood on the High Street overlooking the vicarage road, appears to have been the principal clearinghouse for village information. Over the years this establishment had several different shop assistants and delivery boys, all of whom were called Fred. It becomes confusing to sort out all these young Freds, but we can be sure that at least two of them were different people—Fred Jackson in *The Murder at the Vicarage* and Fred Tyler, recalled by Miss Marple in *A Murder Is Announced*. The main function of these young men seems to have been to court girls and distribute the news of the latest felony, along with the kippers and herrings, around the village. In "Tape-Measure Murder," Miss Marple uttered two words, "The fish," in reply to Constable Palk's demand of how, within half an hour of the discovery of the body, she had learned of a murder. Many years later, in *A Pocket Full of Rye*, the incumbent Fred of that day was to be the innocent cause of Miss Marple's maid, Gladys, leaving the village for another post and a dreadful fate. One cannot help but hope that she had a few moments of happiness before realizing young Fred was not really interested—perhaps in the mysterious room over the fishmonger's, which Miss Wetherby once roguishly hinted about to the Vicar. "I now know," he wrote resignedly, "where maids go on their days out."

The butcher, genial Mr. Murdoch, employed a delivery boy as well, but he never appears to have built up the same following as young Fred. In this establishment it was Mr. Murdoch who seems to have acquired a rather amorous reputation, though "some people said it was just gossip, and that Mr. Murdoch himself liked to encourage the rumours!"

Mr. Golden, the baker, had a van as well as a delivery boy; in "The Case of the Caretaker" its door was taken off to serve as a stretcher for the murder victim. Mr. Golden also had an ambitious daughter, Jessie, who left St. Mary Mead to work as a nursery governess and married the son of the house, who was home on leave from India.

Barnes, the grocer, was a favorite of the old guard and, much to Miss Marple's relief, his shop was to remain unchanged for the next thirty years. "So *obliging*, comfortable chairs to sit in by the counter, and cosy discussions as to cuts of bacon, and varieties of cheese." The greengrocer, however, was another story. In *The Murder at the Vicarage* we find that he was "not behaving at all nicely with the chemist's wife," which was not surprising, considering that the chemist's shop always seemed to be in a state of marital upheaval.

The chemist, whose wife enjoyed the attentions of the

greengrocer, rejoiced in the name of Cherubim. One of Mr. Cherubim's predecessors, a Mr. Badger, was recalled by Miss Marple in *The Body in the Library*. He "made a lot of fuss over the young lady who worked in his cosmetics section. Told his wife they must look on her as a daughter and have her live in the house." So infatuated did Mr. Badger become that he spent a lot of his savings on a diamond bracelet and radio-gramophone for the girl, until he discovered that she was carrying on with another man. Despite this setback Mr. Badger seems to have gone from strength to strength, for we next hear of him as a supposed widower in "The Herb of Death" with:

> ". . . a very young housekeeper—young enough to be not only his daughter but his granddaughter. Not a word to anyone, and his family, a lot of nephews and nieces, full of expectations. And when he died, would you believe it, he'd been secretly married to her for two years?"

The wool shop was run by Mrs. Cray, who was "devoted to her son, spoilt him, of course. He got in with a very queer lot." The paper shop was run by Mrs. Pusey, whose nephew "brought home stuff he'd stolen and got her to dispose of it. . . . And when the police came round and started asking questions, he tried to bash her on the head." Longdon's, the draper's, was where Miss Marple had her curtains made up; Mrs. Jameson, who "turned you out with a nice firm perm," did her hair; and Miss Politt, who lived above the post office and was a principal in "Tape-Measure Murder," was her dressmaker.

St. Mary Mead also had a builder named Cargill who "bluffed a lot of people into having things done to their houses they never meant to do"; an automobile mechanic named Jenkins who was none too honest over batteries; and a vet, Mr. Quinton, whose peccadilloes, if any, have gone unrecorded.

One of the most venerable institutions in the village was Inch's Taxi Service. It had been started by Mr. Inch many years before in the days of horse and cab and, though it had long since graduated to motorcars and other owners, it always retained the name of Inch. The older ladies of St. Mary Mead invariably referred to their journeys by taxi as "going somewhere 'in Inch,' as though they were Jonah and Inch was a whale."

The post office stood at the crossroads on a corner opposite the church. The postman was absent-minded and so was the postmistress. Griselda once teased her husband:

"Oh! Len, you adore me. Do you remember that day when I stayed up in town and sent you a wire you never got because the postmistress's sister was having twins and she forgot to send it round? The state you got into, and you telephoned Scotland Yard and made the most frightful fuss."

Wrote the Vicar gloomily, "There are things one hates being reminded of."

The afternoon arrival, more or less precisely at two-thirty, of the Much Benham bus at the post office was one of the events of the day in St. Mary Mead. Mrs. Blade, the postmistress, could be counted on to hurry out to meet it, thus leaving the public telephone unattended for some four minutes, an important fact that helped Miss Marple solve the "Tape-Measure Murder."

On the other side of the crossroads stood the village pub, the Blue Boar. The first landlord we learn of was Joe Bucknell. "Such a to-do about his daughter carrying on with young Bailey," Miss Marple once recalled. "And all the time it was that minx of a wife of his." Just when the Bucknells left St. Mary Mead is uncertain, but their most memorable successors were the Emmotts. Tom Emmott, "a big burly man of middle age with a shifty eye and a truculent jaw," was a bit of a blackguard in Colonel Melchett's opinion. Like Joe Bucknell, he had family problems. His pretty, wayward daughter, Rose, came to an untimely end in the river just below the Mill.

The Blue Boar, like so many other landmarks in St. Mary Mead, had some atypical uses. It was a good place to have been seen drinking in, for example, at the moment a murder was supposed to have taken place. It was a comfortable home away from home for visiting chief constables and Scotland Yard inspectors. ("The Blue Boar gives you a first-rate meal of the joint-and-two-vegetable type," the Vicar once told Colonel Melchett wistfully.) When the need arose, it was the most appropriate place in St. Mary Mead in which to hold an inquest.

The railway station stood at the opposite end of the village on the branch line to Much Benham. Feelings could run high, and alibis could be overturned, if the trains ran late, a not unusual occurrence. To go up to London (the Thursday cheap return was the favorite excursion), one could catch the morning train or have an early lunch and travel by the 12:15. In either case one had to change at the junction at Much Benham. The evening 6:50 was a popular train on which to come home. If one returned after midnight to find the last train on the branch line to St. Mary Mead gone, one could take a taxi from Much Benham—but not, one hopes, to one's death, as did poor Giuseppe, the Italian butler at Gossington Hall.

To be the resident constable at the St. Mary Mead police station must have been an interesting posting. Was it vied for, perhaps, as an important advancement, or meted out as a punishment, like being sent to the Russian Front? Whatever the case, Constable Hurst of *The Murder at the Vicarage* was described as looking "very important but slightly worried," and Constable Palk of "Tape-Measure Murder" and *The Body in the Library* seems to have developed a nervous habit of sucking his moustache. One would have thought, looking back, that one of the advantages of the position would have been the opportunity of working closely with Miss Marple, but, ungratefully enough, the first place these constables invariably seemed to have turned for help was the county police headquarters in Much Benham, presided over by Miss Marple's old antagonist, Inspector Slack. "Inspector Slack? Police Constable Palk here. A report has just come in that the body of a young woman was discovered this morning at seven-fifteen"—and the hunt would be up, and the big guns would start to arrive.

St. Mary Mead came into Much Benham's domain in

many other ways as well. It was there that Colonel Melchett, the county's chief constable, and Dr. Roberts, the coroner, had their offices; it was there, at the mortuary, that one went to view unidentified bodies (brandy was available); it was there, if one was taken ill or met with an accident, that one was rushed to the hospital; it was there, if one was Colonel Bantry, that one went to meetings of the Conservative Association; it was there, if one was Mrs. Price Ridley, that one bought one's formidable hats; it was there, if one had old silver to appraise, that one went to "a very good man"; it was there, if one was Griselda, that one went secretly to purchase books on Mother-Lore (only to be discovered in the act of doing so by Miss Marple). "Our adjoining town" the villagers called it, but Much Benham, larger and only two miles away, must have privately regarded St. Mary Mead as a potential, if somewhat troublesome, suburb.

Besides popping over to Much Benham, running up to London, calling in for tea, dropping by the Blue Boar, or lending a hand with the parish activities, what else did the inhabitants of St. Mary Mead do with their apparently plentiful leisure time? If one was so inclined, one could go to the cinema, attend the Bingo Club, or play "village bridge." If one was energetic, one could patronize the golf links or play tennis. If one was more sedentary, one could garden, bird watch, or visit the lending library. But above all, if one was an inhabitant of St. Mary Mead, much of one's time was taken up by crime—as either a perpetrator, victim, or spectator thereof—for it is a fact that, over the years, the number of crimes, particularly homicides, committed within the borders of this one small English village appears to have reached an extraordinarily high level in proportion to its modest size.

Consider the record. A search through Marpelian literature will reveal that over a period of some forty years, there occurred in St. Mary Mead a total of sixteen murders—five by poisoning, two by shooting, two by drowning, two by strangling, and five by unidentified means—plus four attempts at murder by poisoning, smothering, and bashing on the head. In the same period there occurred five robberies, eight embezzlements, two series of blackmailing, several illegal impersonations, a case or two of poaching, and a number of crank phone calls, poison-pen letters, and criminal libels. Faced with these statistics, one cannot help but count St. Mary Mead fortunate in having had, in the same period of time, a resident sleuth of the stature of Miss Marple. Without her indomitable presence, where would it all have ended? Characteristically, she herself took a modest view of her accomplishments: "Very nasty things go on in a village, I assure you," she once murmured. "One has an opportunity of studying things there that one would never have in town."

Thus St. Mary Mead about the year 1935. Periodically, in the years to follow, Miss Marple would be heard to complain that "St. Mary Mead was *not* the place it had been," but to revisit it in the fifties, sixties, and seventies was to find many of its inhabitants and institutions older but reassuringly unchanged. Miss Wetherby, alas, "had passed on and her house was now inhabited by the bank manager and his family, having been given a face-lift by the painting of doors and windows a bright royal blue," and Mrs. Price Ridley had faded from the scene, but Miss Hartnell's stentorian voice was still to be heard "fighting progress to the last gasp," and Dr. Haydock, now elderly and semi-retired, still called upon Miss Marple to prescribe a "nice juicy murder" as her best tonic. Though Mrs. Jameson, the hairdresser, "had steeled herself to going as far in the cause of progress as to repaint her sign and call herself 'DIANE. HAIR STYLIST.' . . . the shop remained much as before and catered in much the same way to the needs of the clients," while elsewhere on the High Street, the most recent scandal concerning the chemist's wife continued to hold the village's attention. Old ladies could still depend on faithful Inch, and while there were new faces at the St. Mary Mead and Much Benham police stations, their owners seemed as incapable of preventing the less attractive members of the community from murdering or being murdered as had their predecessors.

Nevertheless, some real changes did occur in St. Mary Mead in those postwar decades: the building of the new Development, for example, and the wave of outsiders it brought with it; the alterations to the High Street; the arrival of a glittering new supermarket; and the rather frightening proximity of an airfield (a jet plane once broke the sound barrier and two windows in Miss Marple's greenhouse at the same time). All these were radical departures from the past. Next door to Miss Marple, an even more profound change occurred with the departure of the Clements and the arrival of a new, and even more absentminded, vicar.

Perhaps the most interesting changes of all were the ones that took place at Gossington Hall. Following the death of Colonel Bantry, Mrs. Bantry, who became as comfortable and cheerful a widow as she had been a wife, sold Gossington Hall, keeping the East Lodge for herself. Cast adrift, Gossington Hall had a checkered career reminiscent of Old Hall in the 1930s. First run as an unsuccessful guest house, it was then

> bought by four people who had shared it as four roughly divided flats and subsequently quarrelled. Finally the Ministry of Health had bought it for some obscure purpose for which they eventually did not want it.

The next owner was far more exciting, easily the most glamorous outsider ever to alight in St. Mary Mead. A film star of international repute, Marina Gregg arrived in the village with her fifth husband and a retinue of assorted eccentrics to live in a fabulously renovated Gossington Hall. Tarted up, it once again proved a splendid place for bodies. Three, possibly four, sensational killings in quick succession were enough to set a village, even one as experienced as St. Mary Mead, completely agog.

And what of St. Mary Mead today? Does an Arab sheik now preside over the palm court and pool at Gossington Hall? If so, what is his imminent fate? As Development follows Development, will St. Mary Mead disappear entirely into the boundaries of an unsuspecting Much Benham? Has a judicial inquiry been appointed, or a Royal Commission struck, to investigate the uncontrollable rise in village crime since the sad departure of its resident Nemesis?

"I regard St. Mary Mead as a stagnant pool," Miss Marple's sophisticated young nephew once remarked.

"That is really not a very good simile, dear Raymond," his aunt replied briskly. "Nothing, I believe, is so full of life under the microscope as a drop of water from a stagnant pool."

Two

Miss Marple's Earlier Life

"I live very quietly in the country, you see."
—Miss Marple, *Nemesis*

M iss Marple was born at the age of sixty-five to seventy—which, as with Poirot, proved most unfortunate, because she was going to have to last a long time in my life," wrote Agatha Christie in her autobiography. Embryonically, Miss Marple may have had some early relationship to Caroline, the doctor's sister in *The Murder of Roger Ackroyd*, which was published four years before the first appearance of Miss Marple. Of Caroline, Dr. Sheppard said:

> "The motto of the mongoose family, so Mr. Kipling tells us, is: 'Go and find out.' If Caroline ever adopts a crest, I should certainly suggest a mongoose rampant. One might

omit the first part of the motto. Caroline can do any amount of finding out by sitting placidly at home. I don't know how she manages it, but there it is."

Agatha Christie was fond of Caroline, and when, in an adaptation of *Roger Ackroyd* to the stage, she was replaced by a young, attractive girl, she resented her removal very much: "I liked the part she played in village life. . . . I think at that moment, in St. Mary Mead, though I did not yet know it, Miss Marple was born."*

Agatha Christie's grandmother and her friends provided further inspiration. Miss Marple was, in Agatha Christie's words,

> the sort of old lady who would have been rather like some of my grandmother's Ealing cronies—old ladies whom I have met in so many villages where I have gone to stay as a girl. Miss Marple was not in any way a picture of my grandmother; she was far more fussy and spinsterish than my grandmother ever was. But one thing she did have in common with her—though a cheerful person, she always expected the worst of everyone and everything, and was, with almost frightening accuracy, usually proved right.

Despite Miss Marple's first appearance as a detective at the age of sixty-five or thereabouts, it is possible to piece together something of her childhood and girlhood from clues she occasionally dropped in conversation dur-

* It is interesting to recall that Caroline Sheppard, Miss Marple's progenitor, had, for a short and interesting time, Hercule Poirot as a neighbor, a person whom Miss Marple herself apparently never met.

ing her extraordinarily long old age. Characteristically, she had from the beginning an excellent memory: "I've always remembered the mauve irises on my nursery walls and yet I believe it was re-papered when I was only three." On this wallpaper, over her bed, was pinned a prophetic text: *Ask and you shall receive.*

There was probably only one other child in the nursery, a sister, and the two little girls seem to have spent the sort of strict, sheltered, governess-run lives familiar to us from the first chapters of many Victorian autobiographies.

There are reports of long hours in the schoolroom. In old age Miss Marple knew very well how hard it was for youth to picture her "young and pigtailed and struggling with decimals and English literature," but adds, wryly, "I was, I think, well educated for the standard of my day. My sister and I had a German governess—a Fräulein. A very sentimental creature. She taught us the language of flowers." This mild disrespect for the kind of education girls of her time received was once confided to, of all people, her old enemy, Inspector Slack:

> "So difficult, you know, to explain oneself, don't you think? . . . not having been educated in the modern style—just a governess, you know, who taught one the dates of the Kings of England and General Knowledge . . . Discursive, you know, but not teaching one to keep to the point."

To her great ally, Inspector Craddock, when he spoke admiringly of the women of her generation, she replied:

I'm sure, my dear boy, you would find the young lady of the type you refer to as a very inadequate helpmeet nowadays. Young ladies were not encouraged to be intellectual and very few of them had university degrees or any kind of academic distinction.

There were many *dos* and *don'ts*: "Miss Marple sat very upright because she had been taught to use a back-board as a girl"; "In my young days it was considered to be very bad manners to take medicines with one's meals. It was on a par with blowing your nose at the dinner table"; "When I was a girl, Inspector, nobody ever mentioned the word stomach."

But there were useful compensations: riddles and Mother Goose rhymes in early childhood, playing with disappearing ink, conjuring tricks ("It was the trick of the Lady Sawn in Half that made me think of it," she was to say many years later to a bemused Inspector Curry), and visits to Madame Tussaud's.

Who were her parents, and where did they live? We are never told exactly, but a distinctly clerical pattern, almost Mafia-like in its family connections, seems to emerge. Miss Marple was, we do know, a "pink and white English girl from a Cathedral Close" and probably, therefore, the daughter of a canon or the dean of a cathedral. One of the few mentions of her father was of him bringing home bronzes purchased at the Paris Exhibition. We are also given a glimpse of Miss Marple's mother and grandmother in Paris:

"We went to have tea at the Elysée Hotel. And my grandmother looked round, and she said suddenly, 'Clara,

I do believe I am the only woman here in a *bonnet!*' And she was, too! When she got home she packed up all her bonnets, and her beaded mantles too—and sent them off."

It is clear that these two, her mother and grandmother, undertook to initiate Miss Marple at an early age into the obligations and mysteries of being a lady. "To wit: that a true lady can neither be shocked nor surprised"; that "a gentlewoman should always be able to control herself in public, however much she may give way in private"; and, above all, that a lady must always do her duty: "Port wine jelly and calf's head broth taken to the sick. My mother used to do it."

In later years Miss Marple was to speak of "the old days, with all the big family reunions." At such gatherings there were no doubt assembled her aunts: her Great Aunt Fanny, for example, who told Miss Marple when she was sixteen that "young people think the old people are fools— but the old people *know* the young people are fools!"; her Aunt Helen who, perhaps because she had never been to Paris, would probably arrive wearing a bonnet and what she always called her "black poplin" mantle; the survivor aunt, whose name we do not know, who had been shipwrecked on five different occasions; and the detective aunt, no doubt a significant early model, who could smell when people told lies, because "their noses twitched, she said, and then the smell came."

Also arriving would be the uncles: Great Uncle Thomas, the retired admiral, who lived in a handsome terrace in Richmond; Uncle Henry, the bachelor, described on one occasion as "a man of unusual self-control," and on another as someone who was given to temper tantrums over food and a habit of keeping a great deal of money hidden in his library behind volumes of sermons. And then would come the canons: the uncle who was a canon of Chichester Cathedral, and Uncle Thomas, who was a canon of Ely.

Her cousins, Anthony and Gordon, would probably be there as well. "Whatever Anthony did always went right for him, and with poor Gordon it was just the other way about; race horses went lame, and stocks went down." Cousin Fanny Godfrey, who stuttered, would no doubt be present, and perhaps Cousin Ethel, Lady Merridew, who lived in style in Lowndes Square. Many years later Miss Marple was to gaze upon a painful scene—a vast skyscraper of modern design built upon the site where Lady Merridew's house once stood. "There must *be* progress I suppose," mused Miss Marple. "If Cousin Ethel knew, she'd turn in her grave, I'm sure."

At fourteen Miss Marple was given a great treat—a visit to London with her Aunt Helen and Uncle Thomas, the Canon of Ely, to stay at Bertram's Hotel. Forever after, Bertram's, "dignified, unostentatious and quietly expensive," was to remain in Miss Marple's mind as the ultimate holiday. It was probably during a visit such as this that a pilgrimage was made across Battersea Bridge to visit a retired governess, Miss Ledbury, who lived at Princes Terrace Mansions, and it was almost certainly the occasion for one of her Aunt Helen's memorable expeditions, niece in tow, to the grocery department of the Army & Navy Stores, there to seek out "our special man" from whom to order, in an ensuing leisurely hour,

> every conceivable grocery that could be purchased and stored up for future use. Christmas was provided for, and there was even a far-off look towards Easter. The young Jane had fidgeted somewhat, and been told to go and look at the glass department by way of amusement. . . . Having had a thoroughly pleasant morning, Aunt Helen would say in the playful manner of those times "And how would a little girl feel about some luncheon." Whereupon they went up in the lift to the fourth floor and had luncheon which always finished with a strawberry ice.

To round off her education, Miss Marple was sent, at about the age of sixteen, to school in Florence. There she met two American girls, Ruth and Carrie Louise Martin, "exciting to the English girl because of their quaint ways of speech and their forthright manner and vitality." They were to become her lifelong friends. "In spite of all my aches and pains," Carrie Louise was to say to Miss Marple nearly fifty years later, "It seems only a few months ago that we were at Florence. Do you remember Fräulein Schweich and her boots?"

"Of course it was the fashion when we were young to have ideals," Carrie's sister, Ruth, once said to Miss Marple.

> "We all had them, it was the proper thing for young girls. You were going to nurse lepers, Jane, and I was going to be a nun. One gets over all that nonsense. Marriage, I suppose one might say, knocks it out of one.

Still, taking it by and large, I haven't done badly out of marriage."

Neither did Carrie Louise. Between them the two sisters were to acquire six husbands and a great deal of wealth. It can hardly be said that Miss Marple followed their examples.

Though she herself did not marry and was destined, in fact, to become the archetypal village spinster, Miss Marple had her own salad days and a number of beaux. In old age she was to recall them with indulgence:

> Jane Marple, that pink and white eager young girl. . . . Such a silly girl in many ways . . . now who was that very unsuitable young man whose name—oh dear, she couldn't even remember it now! How wise her mother had been to nip that friendship so firmly in the bud. She had come across him years later—and really he was quite dreadful! At the time she had cried herself to sleep for at least a week!

And there was:

> A young man she had met at a croquet party. He had seemed so nice—rather gay, almost *Bohemian* in his views. And then he had been unexpectedly warmly welcomed by her father. He had been suitable, eligible; he had been asked freely to the house more than once, and Miss Marple had found that, after all, he was *dull*. Very dull.

And she had enjoyed dancing. In old age, holidaying in the Caribbean, she would have preferred "the muted strains of the 'Blue Danube,' " though she had to confess that watching the local dancing had its merits as well:

"She liked the shuffling feet and the rhythmic sway of the bodies." Rather more comfortable, perhaps, than

> "dancing with a man dressed as a brigand chief when I was a young girl. He had five kinds of knives and daggers, and I can't tell you how awkward and uncomfortable it was for his partner."

In later years, when she was in her sixties, seventies, and eighties, Miss Marple occasionally made such references to her girlhood, but on no recorded occasion did she ever refer directly to all the other years between. We know nothing of her life as a young woman, her middle age, or how she came to her appointed place as the resident sleuth of St. Mary Mead. One would like to speculate, to imagine something vaguely heroic, perhaps, but it is all explained as much as it will ever be, I suspect, by scattered references to home nursing. "I am used to sick people," she once said. "I have had a great deal to do with them in my time." On another occasion we are told: "Long experience of nursing made Miss Marple almost automatically straighten the sheet and tuck it under the mattress on her side of the bed."

"Long experience of nursing . . ." From this single phrase emerges a picture of the unmarried daughter, the once pink-and-white eager girl, who stayed at home in some provincial town to gradually become, as the years passed, the companion and nurse of her parents in their old age. She also became, as we shall see, the real or honorary favorite aunt—sometimes doting, sometimes vinegary—of a number of people.

Few would regard all this as an exciting life, but nowhere is there any hint that Miss Marple considered herself a martyr. She did, however, once confide to a lonely person:

> "I know what you mean. . . . One *is* alone when the last one who *remembers* is gone. I have nephews and nieces and kind friends—but there's no one who belongs to the old days. I've been alone for quite a long time now."

Behold her, then: Miss Jane Marple, her parents dead, her sister dead, her jolly aunts and uncles long gone to their proper rest. She is living alone in genteel and thrifty old age in the quiet village of St. Mary Mead, the possessor of a small but pretty Victorian house no doubt purchased from a modest inheritance left her some years before by her dear parents.

It is the 1930s—or is it the 1920s?—and she is about to embark on an amazing career.

Three

Miss Marple's Career Begins

"It is true, of course, that I have lived what is called a very uneventful life, but I have had a lot of experiences in solving different little problems that have arisen."

—Miss Marple, "The Thumbmark of St. Peter"

Attempting to pinpoint Miss Marple's age at any particular time during the ensuing forty or so years is as baffling as any of her cases. If one begins, for example, with Agatha Christie's statement "Miss Marple was born at the age of sixty-five to seventy" in referring to her first appearance in *The Murder at the Vicarage*, published in 1930, and ends the sum with the certainty that her last recorded case was *Nemesis*, published in 1971, one is forced to conclude that Miss Marple was still going strong, albeit tottery, at anywhere from the age of one hundred and six to one hundred and eleven. Or if, for example, one pounces on Miss Marple's and Carrie Louise Serrocold's reminiscences in *Murder With Mirrors*, published in 1952, about "events that had happened nearly half a century ago" and carries them away to do arithmetic on the assumption that Miss Marple and Carrie Louise were sixteen at the time, one is led to believe that in the early 1950s, more than twenty years after *The Murder at the Vicarage*, Miss Marple is still only about sixty-five. There are a number of such conundrums in Marpelian literature, each of them as contradictory. "*I* look every minute of *my* age!" Miss Marple once said. But what was it as she said it? We never really know.

An even greater challenge is to try and reconcile chronologically the events in Miss Marple's life with the order in which the accounts of her adventures were written and published. Putting aside for the moment her debut in *The Murder at the Vicarage*, the Miss Marple of some of the short stories published in the late 1930s appears to be very much older and Victorian than she ever will be again.

She had on black lace mittens, and a black lace cap surmounted the piled-up masses of her snowy hair. She was knitting—something white and soft and fleecy. Her faded blue eyes, benignant and kindly, surveyed her nephew and her nephew's guests with gentle pleasure.

Contrast this picture with what Crump, the butler in *A Pocket Full of Rye*, saw some twenty years later.

> . . . a tall, elderly lady wearing an old-fashioned tweed coat and skirt, a couple of scarves and a small felt hat with a bird's wing. The old lady carried a capacious handbag and an aged but good-quality suitcase reposed by her feet.

To complicate things even more, the elderly, stay-at-home Miss Marple of the daguerreotypic black lace mittens and cap takes part in events that clearly happen well before the much later adventures of the old but comparatively younger lady of the tweed suit of the 1950s, and even before those of the brisk and spidery Miss Marple of the very first full-length book, *The Murder at the Vicarage*. Examples of this sort of contradiction abound, especially in the chronicles of the 1930s.

But do these contradictions matter? She was, after all, a superb actress, required by her ingenious creator to be an old lady for all seasons. Still, as Miss Marple herself once said, "It's so nice to get people sorted out." In an attempt to do this, let us proceed to her remarkable career, beginning at what appears to be the beginning and proceeding from case to case regardless of when they actually appeared in print.

Assuming that every true professional must serve an apprenticeship, full credit must be given to the village of St. Mary Mead for providing the training ground that was to produce one of the finest detectives of our time. Who cut the meshes of Mrs. Jones's string bag? Why did

Mrs. Sims wear her new fur coat only once? What could explain the curious behavior of Mr. Selkirk's delivery van? Who stole Miss Wetherby's gill of picked shrimps? Long before the outset of that remarkable era that was to see so many of her circle of acquaintances extinguished by fatal accidents, Miss Marple was to spend many edifying years sharpening her wits on mysteries such as these. In the days that were to follow, this great archive of village secrets and misdemeanors, all perfectly filed away in her mind and available at all times, was to prove invaluable. No matter how sensational or complex a murder might be, no matter how far from her home it might be committed, if Miss Marple came to be involved in its solution, it was her invariable practice to hark back immediately to the helpful iniquities and scandals of St. Mary Mead.

"Ah, that reminds me," she would say, or "I have seen so many cases of this kind," and off she would go with reminiscences of Mr. Cargill, the builder, or what the new schoolmistress found when she went to wind up the clock. Often her attendant captive audience, usually a rising young Scotland Yard inspector laboring under the delusion that it was actually he who was in charge of the case, would be left wondering if he was about to go mad.

Was it woman's intuition that accounted for her success? a skeptical admirer once wondered. "No, she doesn't call it that," replied Sir Henry Clithering, a retired ex-Commissioner of Scotland Yard. "Specialized knowledge is her claim. . . . Miss Marple has an interesting, though occasionally trivial, series of parallels from village life."

The Vicar had another name for them. "These unsavory reminiscences," he called them, but they were to stand Miss Marple in excellent stead.

Despite her first published appearance in *The Murder at the Vicarage*, Miss Marple's emergence as a first-class detective really began with the Tuesday Night Club short stories, which appear to take place much earlier in time. It is in a number of these that we find the curiously dated Miss Marple of the black lace mittens and cap.

The Tuesday Night Club, a group of six, appears to have grown out of what Griselda Clement would later call a "Nephew-Amusing Party," an occasion that was apt to occur whenever Miss Marple was honored by a visit from her clever and patronizing nephew, Raymond West, a rising young novelist and poet. Assembled to entertain him on this particular occasion in Miss Marple's drawing room were Sir Henry Clithering; Joyce Lemprière, the artist, an interesting young woman with a "close-cropped black head and queer hazel-green eyes"; Mr. Petherick, the solicitor, "a dried-up little man with eyeglasses"; and Dr. Pender, St. Mary Mead's elderly clergyman, presumably Rev. Leonard Clement's predecessor.

It is reasonable to suppose that the sophisticated Sir Henry Clithering and Joyce Lemprière were invited by Raymond West, with Miss Marple adding her own friends, Dr. Pender and Mr. Petherick, but, however assembled, they all got on famously, and the conversation soon turned to unsolved crimes. It would seem, they quickly agreed, that no better group than themselves could be found to

tackle such problems—after all, as Joyce Lemprière en-
thusiastically pointed out, as a committee combining her
own artistic and feminine intuition with Raymond West's
imagination, Mr. Petherick's ability to sift evidence im-
partially, Dr. Pender's knowledge of human character,
and Sir Henry's experience of the criminal mind, how
could they fail?

"You have forgotten me, dear," said Miss Marple, smiling brightly.

Joyce was slightly taken aback, but she concealed the
fact quickly.

"That would be lovely, Miss Marple," she said.

And so they began, with Sir Henry Clithering describing
an unsolved murder but withholding its solution, which
had just come to his knowledge through a deathbed
confession.

Thus was born, in a short story of the same name, the
Tuesday Night Club, which met regularly until each
member in turn had presented an unsolved crime from
his own experience for the others to solve. The pattern
of these pleasant evenings never varied. At this first
meeting, for example, Joyce Lemprière, Mr. Petherick,
Raymond West, and Dr. Pender collectively dissected
and discussed every intelligible aspect of the problem Sir
Henry Clithering had posed, occasionally interrupted by
their elderly hostess's irrelevant musings on village life.
At length they arrived at four different conclusions, all
of them, as it turned out, quite wrong.

"And now Sir Henry, tell us," said Joyce eagerly.

"One moment," said Sir Henry. "Miss Marple has not yet spoken."

"Dear, dear," she said. "I have dropped another stitch. I have been so interested in the story. A sad case, a very sad case. It reminds me of old Mr. Hargraves who lived up at the Mount."

And off she goes, rambling away about maids and desserts and dead-and-gone Hargraves until—snap—there, laid before them all, is the solution.

The eyes of the others were all fixed upon Sir Henry.

"It is a very curious thing," he said slowly, "but Miss Marple happens to have hit upon the truth."

So passed the next four meetings of the Tuesday Night Club, with Miss Marple, to the amazement of her audience, neatly solving every case: Dr. Pender's "The Idol House of Astarte," a rambling tale of archaeological mumbo jumbo (no problem if "one looks at the facts and disregards all that atmosphere of heathen goddesses which I don't think is very nice"); Raymond West's swashbuckling "Ingots of Gold" ("Well, he can't have been a real gardener, can he? . . . Gardeners don't work on Whit Monday"); Joyce Lemprière's sinister "The Bloodstained Pavement" ("Sitting here with one's knitting, one just sees the facts"); Mr. Petherick's ingenious "Motive v. Opportunity" ("Disappearing ink . . . Many is the time I have played with it as a child"); and, of course, her own story, "The Thumbmark of St. Peter" ("I connected the two things together, faith—and fish").

It is interesting to pause over "The Thumbmark of St.

Peter," a story set ten or fifteen years before the telling, because in it Miss Marple describes what may well be the first murder case she ever solved.

"One, two, three, four, five, and then three purl; that is right. Now, what was I saying? Oh yes, about poor Mabel." "Poor Mabel" was Miss Marple's niece, a rather tiresome though good-hearted girl whose disagreeable husband had died under such peculiar circumstances that she was in danger of being ostracized by all her friends and neighbors. Mabel may have been silly and in a nervous state, but she obviously had just enough good sense to appeal to the right person for help, her Aunt Jane.

It is fascinating to watch Miss Marple embark upon this case, a curtain raiser for so many that were to follow: "I put Clara on board wages and sent the plate and the King Charles tankard to the bank, and I went off at once."

When the curtain next rises, we find her hard at work in Mabel's village, briskly collecting the evidence, sifting through the rumors, interviewing the family doctor and the servants, arranging for an autopsy, discussing its outcome with the pathologist, conducting some interesting medical research of her own, and, in all due course, unmasking the murderer. No wonder Sir Henry prophetically declared, at the conclusion of her story, "I shall recommend Scotland Yard to come to you for advice."

So ended the last meeting of the Tuesday Night Club. Presumably Raymond West concluded this particular visit to his Aunt Jane and there was no further need to entertain him. Thanks to Sir Henry Clithering, however, news of Miss Marple's abilities as a first-class detective was about to spread.

"When I was down here last year—" said Sir Henry Clithering, and stopped.

His hostess, Mrs. Bantry, looked at him curiously.

The ex-Commissioner of Scotland Yard was staying with old friends of his, Colonel and Mrs. Bantry, who lived near St. Mary Mead.

Mrs. Bantry, pen in hand, had just asked his advice as to who should be invited to make a sixth guest at dinner that evening.

"Yes?" said Mrs. Bantry encouragingly. "When you were here last year?"

"Tell me," said Sir Henry, "do you know a Miss Marple?"

Mrs. Bantry was surprised. It was the last thing she had expected.

"Know Miss Marple? Who doesn't! The typical old maid of fiction. Quite a dear, but hopelessly behind the times. Do you mean you would like me to ask her to dinner?"

But ask her she did, and such was the success of the evening, once her guests were introduced to the novel game of telling unsolved mysteries of such complexity that only an old lady in black lace mittens and a fichu could solve them, that Mrs. Bantry's dinner parties became a regular event. Besides the Bantrys, Sir Henry, and Miss Marple, the participants in this second series included the beautiful and well-known actress, Jane Helier, and St. Mary Mead's physician of that day, the elderly Dr. Lloyd.

Colonel Bantry began with a ghost story, "The Blue Geranium," which he had been trying to find someone to solve for years. Dr. Lloyd contributed "The Companion," which Sir Henry pronounced "a very bold and perfect crime . . . Almost the perfect crime." Sir Henry himself recounted "The Four Suspects," a case of international espionage that had lain unsolved for years in the files of several police forces. Over her knitting, Miss Marple explained how she had single-handedly brought a wife murderer to justice in "A Christmas Tragedy." Mrs. Bantry recalled a nasty episode of suspected poisoning in "The Herb of Death." Jane Helier, by contributing an inconclusive story, "The Affair at the Bungalow," earned some good advice, later imparted privately, from Miss Marple.

Besides the satisfaction of solving all these cases, another happy result for Miss Marple of these dinner parties at Gossington Hall was the friendship that sprang up between herself and Dolly Bantry. From that time on they were to be firm friends and collaborators.

A corollary to this set of mysteries is the story "Death by Drowning," in which Sir Henry Clithering, again staying with the Bantrys, is enlisted by Miss Marple to help prove her theory as to who murdered pretty Rose Emmott, the daughter of the innkeeper at the Blue Boar. So convinced by this time is Sir Henry of Miss Marple's infallibility in all matters criminal that he quite outrageously butts into the investigations of the local authorities—Inspector Drewitt of the county police and Colonel Melchett, the Chief Constable—to carry her cause. It is worth taking note of Colonel Melchett, "a little man of aggressively military demeanour," in this story because he, like Sir Henry Clithering, was to figure in a number of Miss Marple's cases.

Another accomplishment of Miss Marple's that seems to have occurred during this particularly pleasant time of the fireside guessing games was the aid she gave to Mr. Petherick in "Miss Marple Tells A Story." Mr. Petherick, as will be recalled, was St. Mary Mead's shrewd and elderly solicitor and a member of the Tuesday Night Club. In this beautifully constructed little story, it is clear that Miss Marple has by now become something of a consultant, because to her drawing room one evening Mr. Petherick brings a seemingly hopeless case, a client under such grave suspicion of murdering his wife that even the eminent barrister retained to defend him has failed to come up with a reasonable defense. Miss Marple asks Mr. Petherick to outline the known facts, surveys them in all their contradictions, concludes that the client is innocent, and briskly indicates who is not.

Nor was Mr. Petherick the only one to seek out her advice as a result of the guessing games. In "Strange Jest,"* Jane Helier, the beautiful actress who had been one of Mrs. Bantry's dinner guests, introduces Miss Marple to two depressed young people who have been left a fortune by a mischievous uncle but, despite digging up much of his garden and even the flagstones of his cellar,

* First published in *This Week Magazine* under the title "A Case of Buried Treasure."

can't find it. Miss Marple, with considerable twittering, does.

Champagne is drunk to celebrate the happy resolution of the puzzle, and this little occasion also marks the end of Miss Marple's apprenticeship. From this time on we generally find her engaged in much longer cases, with a complete book devoted to each one. To mark this transition, I imagine her thoughtfully packing away her fichu and black lace mittens and embarking on a series of small household economies designed to earn her the price of a pair of really good binoculars.

Four

The 1930s

"There is no detective in England equal to a spinster lady of uncertain age with plenty of time on her hands."

> —Rev. Leonard Clement, *The Murder at the Vicarage*

I t is difficult to know quite where to begin this story, but I have fixed my choice on a certain Wednesday at luncheon at the Vicarage." So begins a narrative penned by the Reverend Leonard Clement on the strange events that occurred in his parish during a memorable high summer of a year in the late 1920s.

For all who love Miss Marple, *The Murder at the Vicarage* holds a special place. Not only is it the first full-length Miss Marple mystery, but in its character and plot it is one of the most endearing and ingenious. Its setting is St. Mary Mead at its archetypal meddling best—the village rivalries, the idiosyncrasies, the caste systems, the deceptive decorum of long summer afternoons with the ladies at their tea and scandal, the young people at their tennis parties, the maids and errand boys courting at the back doors, and a handsome visiting artist up to God knows what in the shed in the Vicar's garden.

Until the unlamented end of Colonel Protheroe, slain by unknown hands in the Vicar's own study, who could have imagined what murder, adultery, thievery, and blackmail lay germinating just below the well-tilled surface of St. Mary Mead? And who could have imagined that from a Greek chorus of village spinsters would emerge a rather dithery old lady capable of finding them all out?

The Murder at the Vicarage also provides an introduction to Miss Marple's circle at that time: her charming and disorganized neighbors, the Clements; her spinster colleagues, the jolly, pouncing Miss Hartnell and the gushing, acidulated Miss Wetherby; and her firm friend and adviser, Dr. Haydock. The energetic and overbearing Inspector Slack also makes his first appearance and commits the error, not to be his last, of seriously underestimating Miss Marple. So, initially, does the fierce little Colonel Melchett, Chief Constable of the County of Downshire, who arrives on the scene in ignorance of the fact that it was Miss Marple who had quietly solved, behind the scenes, an earlier St. Mary Mead case of his, "Death by Drowning." We also meet again Miss Marple's patronizing young nephew, Raymond West, for whose entertainment the Tuesday Night Club murders had been unraveled.

Best of all, *The Murder at the Vicarage* gives us a rich slice of Miss Marple's life and times halfway between the two world wars. There are mild hints of changes under way. Concern is expressed over girls who wear brief bathing suits, the difficulties of finding good servants, and pregnant ladies who play golf, but, once the crimes surrounding Colonel Protheroe's extraordinary death have all been solved, life for a spinster lady in St. Mary Mead resumes its Edwardian air.

Though published in 1942, *The Body in the Library** chronologically follows *The Murder at the Vicarage* in Miss Marple's life. In the last chapter of the latter title, Griselda Clement confides to her husband that she is expecting a baby; in *The Body in the Library* this baby is learning to crawl across the hearth rug, an indication that approximately a year and a half has passed between the discovery of one body in the Vicar's study and the discovery of another in Colonel Bantry's library.

According to G.C. Ramsey in *Agatha Christie, Mistress of Mystery*, Christie considered the first chapter of *The Body in the Library* to be her best beginning, and a par-

* In *Cards on the Table*, a Poirot mystery first published in 1936, another of Agatha Christie's sleuths, Mrs. Ariadne Oliver, is introduced as the author of *The Body in the Library*. Obviously Christie, six years later, could not resist writing a book with this title herself.

ticularly pleasant picture of early morning at Gossington Hall is sketched in the opening pages:

> The rattle of the curtain rings on the stairs as the house-maid drew them, the noises of the second housemaid's dustpan and brush in the passage outside . . . the rustle of a print dress, the subdued chink of tea things as the tray was deposited on the table outside, then the soft knock and the entry of Mary to draw the curtains.

On the morning the book begins, however, "there was no chink of curtain rings. Out of the dim green light Mary's voice came, breathless, hysterical. 'Oh, ma'am, oh, ma'am, there's a body in the library!' " A murderer had struck again in St. Mary Mead.

Quickly rushing to the scene are the by now familiar dramatis personae: the rude and "inevitable" Inspector Slack, the shrewd and hot-tempered Colonel Melchett, the blunt and dependable Dr. Haydock, and, in an unofficial capacity, Miss Marple's old friend, Sir Henry Clithering.

It is clear by this time—much to Inspector Slack's discomfiture—that Miss Marple has become something of an acknowledged sleuth. She is the first person Dolly Bantry summons for help following the embarrassing discovery of the strangled body of a beautiful young blonde in her husband's study. "But you're very good at murders," she tells Miss Marple firmly, and Sir Henry says of her to a friend:

> "Downstairs in the lounge, by the third pillar from the left, there sits an old lady with a sweet, placid, spinsterish

face and a mind that has plumbed the depths of human iniquity and taken it as all in the day's work. Her name's Miss Marple. She comes from the village of St. Mary Mead, which is a mile and a half from Gossington; she's a friend of the Bantrys and, where crime is concerned, she's the goods, Conway."

A trio of short stories next advances our knowledge of Miss Marple. Though published in the early 1940s, "Tape-Measure Murder," "The Case of the Perfect Maid," and "The Case of the Caretaker" clearly belong to the 1930s, those happy years of tea and scandal and twittering confrontations with Inspector Slack.

"By the way, have you talked to Miss Marple at all?" asks Colonel Melchett of Inspector Slack in "Tape-Measure Murder,"* following Slack's smug report that the latest crime in St. Mary Mead—Mrs. Spenlow strangled in her sitting room—is an open-and-shut case. Mr. Spenlow did it.

"What's she got to do with it, sir?" objects Slack.

"Oh, nothing," replies the Colonel cautiously, "But she hears things, you know."

And so she has. And so she springs a trap. And so she solves the murder.

"The Case of the Perfect Maid"* is not murder, but in the opinion of Miss Marple's acquaintances it is almost

---

* Also published under the titles "The Case of the Retired Jeweller" and "A Village Murder."

* Also published under the titles "The Maid Who Disappeared" and "The Perfect Maid."

as bad. Servants and their shortcomings are the main topics of conversation in St. Mary Mead, so it is with considerable chagrin that the ladies of the parish see imported into their midst a person purported to be a truly perfect maid—except by Miss Marple, of course, who knew there was no such thing. Small clues to the passage of time are provided by the decline of Old Hall—once the home of the Protheroes in *The Murder at the Vicarage*—into an establishment of four flats, and by mention of the Clements' little boy, now old enough to provide Miss Marple with sticky sweets with which to capture a criminal's fingerprints.

The short story "The Case of the Caretaker" is a present from Dr. Haydock to Miss Marple, one of his favorite patients. On an occasion when she is recovering from a particularly depressing case of flu with no actual murder on hand to distract her, he takes time from his busy practice to write her an unusual prescription, a short whodunit set in St. Mary Mead with a thinly disguised cast of characters. Solving it has Miss Marple feeling better in no time.

A book "I am really pleased with," remarked Agatha Christie in her autobiography, "is *The Moving Finger*. It is a great test to re-read what one has written, some seventeen or eighteen years later. One's view changes. Some do not stand the test of time, others do." *The*

Moving Finger was first published in 1942 but is set in the mid-1930s:

> ". . . but you see, my dear, things are so different now-adays—*taxation*, of course, and then my stocks and shares, so *safe*, as I always imagined, and indeed the bank man-ager *himself* recommended some of them, but they seem to be paying *nothing* at all these days—*foreign*, of course! And really it makes it all so *difficult*."

So mourns Miss Emily Barton, a charming old lady, forced by hard times to rent her comfortable house out to strangers and move to rooms kept by her ex-parlormaid.

The Moving Finger is not set in St. Mary Mead but in Lymstock, an equally picturesque village. Jerry Burton, a prosperous young bachelor convalescing from a flying accident, and his sister Joanna, who "is very pretty and very gay, and . . . likes dancing and cocktails," come to live for a few soothing months of rural calm. The nasty events that follow—obscene letters, suicide, murder, and the general terrorizing of Lymstock—move Jerry, like the Reverend Leonard Clement before him, to write it all down.

Into this lively plot and rudely disturbed village—but only in the last quarter of the book—comes a deceptively subdued and apologetic Miss Marple, summoned by her old friend Mrs. Dane Calthrop, the formidable wife of Lymstock's vicar. As Mrs. Dane Calthrop confides to Jerry, though Scotland Yard may be all very well,

> "I don't mean *that* kind of an expert. I don't mean some-one who knows about anonymous letters or even about

murder. I mean someone who knows *people*. Don't you see? We want someone who knows a great deal about *wickedness!*"

She was right, of course, and as soon as Miss Marple has settled in and taken Lymstock's proper measure, she correctly begins to suspect what nobody else has and neatly solves the case.

Sleeping Murder was published in 1976, the year of Agatha Christie's death, and heralded inaccurately as "Miss Marple's last case." In fact, Christie wrote *Sleeping Murder* and *Curtain,* an Hercule Poirot mystery, as extra books in the early years of the war. "This was in anticipation of my being killed in the raids, which seemed to be in the highest degree likely as I was working in London," she wrote with cheerful good sense in her autobiography. The Miss Marple book was made over by deed of gift to her husband, Max Mallowan, and the Hercule Poirot to her daughter, Rosalind, and for well over thirty years the two mysteries lay in a bank vault, no doubt a favorite family joke.

Curtain really *is* Poirot's last case. Old and frail, he dies, the famous gray cells intact to the end. But *Sleeping Murder* and the Miss Marple in it are quite different. Set in the late 1930s—the King of the day was once the Prince of Wales, and photographs of the Princesses Elizabeth and Margaret Rose stand on a back parlor mantelpiece—Miss Marple is in very good form indeed, her only hint of illness being a bogus one, a ladylike taking to her bed to persuade Dr. Haydock to order her off to the seaside for some bracing air. Her motive in all this is to establish an excuse to visit the quiet Devon town of Dillmouth, where Gwenda Reed, a very frightened young friend of her nephew Raymond, is about to embark on an attempt to prove that murder had been done in her house some eighteen years before.

"Can't you *ever* leave murder alone, woman?" demands Dr. Haydock. In return he receives a small prim smile, and off his patient goes to Dillmouth to lodgings recommended by Dolly Bantry.

Much later, with the case nicely broken open, Detective Inspector Primer, assigned to it, spots Miss Marple:

> "Excuse me, Mrs. Reed. That lady wouldn't be a Miss Jane Marple, would she?" . . .
>
> "Yes, that's Miss Marple. She's awfully kind in helping us with the garden."
>
> "Miss Marple," said the Inspector. "*I* see."
>
> And as Gwenda looked at him inquiringly and said, "She's rather a dear," he replied:
>
> "She's a very celebrated lady, is Miss Marple. Got the Chief Constables of at least three counties in her pocket. She's not got my Chief yet, but I dare say that will come."

Five

Postwar Events

Modesty forbade Miss Marple to reply that she
was, by now, quite at home with murder.
                                    —*Murder with Mirrors*

W hat happened to Miss Marple during the Second World War? Whatever her duty was, we
may be sure that she did it very well. Some of
us might like to picture her at home in St. Mary Mead,
knitting indefatigably. Others might like to imagine that
England would have used her talents in more appropriate
and sensitive ways. Perhaps the language imparted by the
German governess of her youth was not wasted after all?
Whatever occurred, we know nothing about it beyond
one or two bland references in later years, and we next
meet Miss Marple in a postwar setting, about ten years
after *Sleeping Murder*, in *A Murder Is Announced*. If any-

thing, she appears somewhat younger than she did before.

A *Murder Is Announced*, Agatha Christie's fiftieth work, was published in 1950, but we can date the year of its setting exactly as 1948, thanks to a reference on the first page to a critical debate that occurred in the United Nations on October 29 of that year.

As far as the village of Chipping Cleghorn was concerned, however, the important event of that day was the appearance in the local *Gazette* of an advertisement that read:

> A murder is announced and will take place on Friday, October 29th at Little Paddocks at 6:30 P.M. Friends please accept this, the only intimation.

Just as announced, at exactly 6:30 P.M. of that extraordinary day, the lights in Miss Letitia Blacklock's drawing room at Little Paddocks go out on an inquisitive assemblage of callers, the door crashes open, revolver shots ring out, and the lights go on to reveal an unknown and dead young man. There follows an excellent story of blackmail and murder.

In later years Miss Marple was to affectionately recall this case as the one in which she first met Detective Inspector Craddock of Scotland Yard, a young man who was to become her favorite police officer and a sort of honorary nephew. It was, in fact, no coincidence that she did meet Inspector Craddock, as he was the godchild of Sir Henry Clithering, who warmly recommended her to him:

"Remember that an elderly unmarried woman who knits and gardens is streets ahead of any detective sergeant. She can tell you what might have happened and what ought to have happened and even what actually *did* happen. And she can tell you why it happened!"

Though skeptical at first, Inspector Craddock was to become one of Miss Marple's greatest admirers and an enthusiastic supporter of what he called her "snooping." That she was able to snoop so providentially in Chipping Cleghorn during the unraveling of the Little Paddocks case was also due to one of her most interesting behavior patterns—staying with old friends in pretty villages where murders were taking place. In this case Miss Marple stays with the daughter of old friends: Bunch Harmon, Miss Marple's favorite godchild, and the cheerful young wife of Chipping Cleghorn's vicar.

There is much talk in *A Murder Is Announced* about austerity and change. References to the recent war come obliquely through complaints about rationing ("I really don't know how people manage to feed big dogs nowadays—I really *don't*"), about fuel shortages (" 'I suppose there was once heaps of coke and coal for everybody?' said Julia with the interest of one hearing about an unknown country") and, of course, about the servant problem ("nowadays unless one has an old Nannie in the family, who will go into the kitchen and do everything, one is simply *sunk*"). Even Miss Marple, usually so philosophical about change, voices her worries to Inspector Craddock:

"Every village and small country place is full of people who've just come and settled there without any ties to bring them. The big houses have been sold, and the cottages have been converted and changed. And people just come—and all you know about them is what they say of themselves. . . . But nobody *knows* any more who any one is."

Fortunately for Miss Marple, by this time Agatha Christie's acknowledged favorite sleuth, the next decade, the 1950s, was to prove a splendid time for exercising her incomparable talents for finding out who people really were.

"My dear, have you seen what Christian Dior is trying to make us wear in the way of skirts?" exclaims glamorous and ageless Ruth Van Rydock to her old and dear school-friend in the opening chapter of *Murder with Mirrors,* [*] published in 1952. But the old schoolfriend, Jane Marple, who was "dressed in rather dowdy black, carried a large shopping bag and looked every inch a lady," had hardly been invited to journey from St. Mary Mead to her friend's expensive hotel suite to discuss fashion. There was much more than Dior on Mrs. Van Rydock's mind. She proposed, in fact, to send Miss Marple down to the country where her sister, Carrie Louise, had got herself into a third and particularly crankish marriage to a philanthropic man devoted to the running of a large establish-

[*] Also published under the title *They Do It with Mirrors.*

ment for the rehabilitation of young criminals ("Juvenile Delinquency—that's what is the rage nowadays"). Something about the whole atmosphere of this strange and confusing place had Mrs. Van Rydock concerned. But how to investigate?

Mrs. Van Rydock paused, eyed Miss Marple rather uneasily, lighted a cigarette, and plunged rather nervously into explanation.

"You'll admit, I'm sure, that things have been difficult in this country since the war, for people with small fixed incomes—for people like you, that is to say, Jane."

"Oh yes, indeed. But for the kindness, the really great kindness of my nephew Raymond, I don't know really where I should be."

"Never mind your nephew. . . . The point, as I put it to Carrie Louise, is that it's just too bad about dear Jane. Really sometimes hardly enough to eat, and of course far too proud ever to appeal to old friends. One couldn't, I said, suggest *money*—but a nice long rest in lovely surroundings, with an old friend and with plenty of nourishing food, and no cares or worries"—Ruth Van Rydock paused and then added defiantly, "Now go on— be mad at me if you want to be."

Miss Marple opened her china blue eyes in gentle surprise.

"But why should I be mad at you, Ruth? A very ingenious and plausible approach."

It was the reaction of a true professional.

A *Pocket Full of Rye*, published in 1953, is an excellent example of what might be called a Miss Marple Knitting

Novel, in which, in a soothing atmosphere of clicking needles and fleecy baby things, she thinks and listens, lets other people talk and, quite literally, hang themselves. It is also a good example of a Miss-Marple-As-Avenger Novel, in which she regards the murderer to be unmasked as a personal antagonist—in this case the contemptuous killer of a pathetic and rather stupid parlormaid, Gladys Martin, an orphan from St. Mary Mead trained for service by Miss Marple herself.

To avenge Gladys, Miss Marple packs up her aged but good-quality suitcase at a moment's notice, leaves her current maid Kitty to get on with the spring cleaning and travels to Yewtree Lodge, a pretentious and tasteless mansion on the outskirts of London and the scene of Gladys's murder. The speed with which this elderly lady insinuates herself, knitting and all, into this perfectly strange household and into the confidence of the police is a tour de force in itself, though it must be acknowledged that in one respect her reputation had preceded her. Says Inspector Neele, in charge of the case:

> "I admit, Miss Marple, that I've heard something about you at the Yard." He smiled, "It seems you're fairly well known there."
>
> "I don't know how it is," fluttered Miss Marple, "but I so often seem to get mixed up in the things that are really *no* concern of mine. Crimes I mean, and peculiar happenings."

Despite her flutterings, Miss Marple continues to move with the times. Thanks, perhaps, to Ruth Van Rydock's conversations of the year before in *A Pocket Full of Rye*, she is obligingly prepared to talk about the new skirts that are being worn in Paris and to cope with a society that dabbles in flying saucers, truth drugs, atomic bombs, and the uncertainties of air travel. In this complicated plot based on an old nursery rhyme, she appears, in fact, to be in particularly good form with, if anything, a heightening of her faculties. At Yewtree Lodge she needs them all as she and Inspector Neele are pitted against a particularly ruthless and wily killer. At the conclusion, when all has been resolved, she feels an understandable surge of triumph—"the triumph some specialist might feel who has successfully reconstructed an extinct animal from a fragment of jawbone and a couple of teeth."

Next follow two short stories, "Sanctuary" and "Greenshaw's Folly." "Sanctuary" is set in Chipping Cleghorn, the scene about five years before of *A Murder Is Announced*. The very likable Bunch Harmon, Miss Marple's goddaughter, discovers an apparent suicide dying on the chancel steps of the village church, and her suspicions about the whole tragedy lead her to consult with "Aunt Jane," who is spending a fortnight in London. Under Miss Marple's tutelage ("Would you have noticed at all, Bunch dear, whether you were followed when you came to London today?"), and with the help of her old friend Inspector Craddock, a very cheeky trap is set to catch two murderers.

The murder in "Greenshaw's Folly" is a real conjurer's trick—now you see it, now you don't. One of the chief characters is Raymond West, Miss Marple's nephew, now "softening a little with the advent of middle age." The years have brought him to a more respectful attitude toward his aunt's unusual talents. "If you want to discuss murder," he says gravely, "you must talk to my Aunt Jane."

In about 1955 Miss Marple suffered an attack of pneumonia, at which time she was nursed back to health by the incomparable Lucy Eyelesbarrow, a much sought after and expensive nurse-housekeeper retained for his aunt by Raymond West. Despite her recovery, the Miss Marple of *What Mrs. McGillicuddy Saw!*,* published in 1957, does not merely look frail—she *is* frail. Alas for her garden, Dr. Haydock has forbidden her to stoop or kneel. She is becoming slightly deaf, and, worst of all, she herself feels old and tired. But who can resist the opening scene of *What Mrs. McGillicuddy Saw!* when, on a late afternoon in December, Mrs. Elspeth McGillicuddy, travelling from London to spend a few days with her old friend Jane Marple, glimpses a tall, dark man strangling a woman in a first-class carriage of a train that briefly runs parallel to hers? "I'm too old for any more adventures," Miss Marple tells herself when tentative inquiries to the police have yielded nothing and Mrs. McGillicuddy has departed for Ceylon, but a pink flush

* Also published under the titles *4.50 from Paddington*, *Eye Witness to Murder*, and *Murder She Said*.

creeps over her face and she begins to marshal her forces. Before they know it, young Leonard Clement (who is very good at maps), her great-nephew David West (who is very good at railways), Lucy Eyelesbarrow (who is very good at everything), her old maidservant, Faithful Florence, and her dear friend Inspector Craddock of Scotland Yard have all been pressed into service. After all, as Miss Marple points out, "Somebody . . . has committed a very successful crime."

It is all worth the effort; *What Mrs. McGillicuddy Saw!* is deservedly one of Miss Marple's—and Christie's—greatest successes. Emma Lathen, in *Agatha Christie, First Lady of Crime,* has quoted figures to suggest that to keep this book in print in the United States has required the chopping down of five thousand acres of woods in Maine every year. Miss Marple, if she had known, would have been horrified—as horrified, perhaps, as she was with another event of these times. " 'I am really very, very sorry,' " she says at the conclusion of this case, "looking as fierce as a fluffy old lady can look, 'that they have abolished capital punishment.' "

Six

The Four Last Cases

"I have a small notebook with me and a Biro pen."

Miss Marple, *Nemesis*

Though Miss Marple's health remained indifferent throughout the 1960s and into the 1970s, her splendid curiosity carried her through four more intricate cases: *The Mirror Crack'd*, *A Caribbean Mystery*, *At Bertram's Hotel*, and *Nemesis*. Though these four books tell us much about the difficulties and frustrations of old age, Miss Marple's ever-increasing frailty does not prevent her from enjoying herself. In three of these four we find her away from home on holiday, and in *Nemesis*, the last, her efforts and intelligence earn her a handsome fee. (And about time, too.) As to her age, who can tell?

Perhaps Lady Selina Hazy, "sixty-five, up from Leicestershire," in *At Bertram's Hotel* comes as close to the truth as anyone with her complacent remark:

"Why I do believe that's old Jane Marple. Thought she was dead years ago. Looks a hundred."

The Mirror Crack'd, * published in 1963, is a St. Mary Mead mystery that spends considerable time documenting the disconcerting changes that have occurred in Miss Marple's own territory in the previous few years. Alas for one's tea and scandal—Miss Wetherby has died, and Griselda and her Vicar have moved away. Alas for one's garden—it must now be surrendered to a jobbing gardener who neglects the sweet peas and the roses in favor of asters and salvias. Alas for one's knitting—one drops stitches. Alas for one's binoculars—they have had to be put away. Alas for the neighboring green fields of yore—an intrusive new Development now sprawls in their place ("Though why everything had to be called a Close she couldn't imagine. Aubrey Close and Longwood Close, and Grandison Close and all the rest of them. Not really Closes at all"). Alas for Faithful Florence and those other nice little maids of the past—in their place is now the irritating and horribly cheerful Miss Knight, a housekeeper/companion provided by dear Raymond ("And how would we fancy a nice cup of Ovaltine? Or Horlicks for

* Published in England in 1962 under the title *The Mirror Crack'd from Side to Side.*

a change?"). Added to such phenomena as television, tranquilizers, and Teddy Boys, it is all almost too much to bear. Indeed, the opening chapter of *The Mirror Crack'd* finds Miss Marple feeling quite depressed.

But read on to discover that, though Colonel Bantry has passed away, Dolly Bantry continues to enjoy life to the full in the prettily renovated East Lodge of Gossington Hall; to learn that Gossington Hall itself now belongs to the celebrated American actress Marina Gregg, and that the faces of movie stars, only glimpsed before in magazines at the hairdresser's, are now to be seen daily in St. Mary Mead; to see Dr. Haydock, now rather elderly himself, sipping Miss Marple's sherry and delivering himself, as always, of the soundest of medical advice: "What I'd prescribe for you is a nice juicy murder." The murders themselves are so sensational as to bring Miss Marple's beloved Inspector Craddock, now Chief Inspector Craddock, down from Scotland Yard. And read, of course, of how Miss Marple triumphs again and rides in the venerable Inch to Gossington Hall to deliver her astonishing verdict as to who murdered whom and why.

"I'd better come with you, hadn't I dear," said Miss Knight. "It won't take me a minute just to slip on outdoor shoes."

"No, thank you," said Miss Marple, firmly. "I'm going by myself. Drive on, Inch."

In the winter following *The Mirror Crack'd,* Miss Marple suffered another bad case of pneumonia, and once again Raymond West stepped in. Much to her—and our—surprise, we next find her contemplating, not the annoying television antennae of the Development, but the deep blue of a Caribbean sea. Papaw, fresh limes, and passion fruit sundaes have become her daily fare. She is holidaying in the West Indies. Ungrateful she certainly is not, but comparisons are inevitable:

> Lovely and warm, yes—and *so* good for her rheumatism—and beautiful scenery, though perhaps—a trifle monotonous? So *many* palm trees. Everything the same every day—never anything *happening*. Not like St. Mary Mead where something was always happening.

Like the good tourist island that it is, however, St. Honoré obligingly provides an appropriate entertainment: a thoroughly English set of murders. Hence *A Caribbean Mystery*, published in 1964.

It is a great pleasure in *A Caribbean Mystery* to find Miss Marple feeling comparatively well, despite her recent bout of pneumonia. Perhaps this is due to an exotic strain of vitamin C in the papaw, but there is no mention in this book of failing eyesight and dropped stitches. While she may move somewhat slowly along the paths of her pleasant hotel and nod off to sleep during the passions of a steel band, it is a very alert Miss Marple indeed who prowls on stockinged feet "with all the care of a Big Game Hunter" in pursuit of a suspect, and who, in the interests of justice, breaks into a sleeping man's hotel room and shakes him violently awake.

In this book Miss Marple acquires an important new admirer and ally, Jason Rafiel. At first sight he hardly seems to qualify as a worthy successor to Sir Henry Clithering and Chief Inspector Craddock ("The principal thing known about Mr. Rafiel was that he was incredibly rich, he came every year to the West Indies, he was semi-paralysed and looked like a wrinkled old bird of prey") but Miss Marple could never have solved the murders in *A Caribbean Mystery* without him. A number of years later, he was to reenter her life in a most surprising way.

The following year the extremely generous Raymond once again treated his aunt to a memorable holiday, a fortnight's stay at London's famous old Bertram's Hotel:

> . . . dignified, unostentatious, and quietly expensive . . . patronised over a long stretch of years by the higher *échelons* of the clergy, dowager ladies of the aristocracy up from the country, girls on their way home for the holidays from expensive finishing schools. ("So few places where a girl can stay alone in London but of course it is *quite* all right at Bertram's. We have stayed there for *years.*")

Miss Marple had stayed there herself as a girl of fourteen and had never forgotten it, which makes *At Bertram's Hotel*, published in 1965, of particular interest from the point of view of biography, because in it she reminisces a good deal about the past and undertakes a number of small excursions to places she knew as a girl. This nostalgia is reinforced by the impeccable Edwardianism of Bertram's, amazingly unchanged over the years except for discreet additions of central heating and modern plumbing. It is all almost too good to be true, thinks Miss Marple, sitting up in bed in her pretty room and eating a cozy breakfast of tea, poached eggs, and rolls. "So adept was the chambermaid that she did not even mention cereals or orange juice."

Miss Marple is right. It *is* all too good to be true, and it is very disconcerting indeed when Canon Pennyfather, a fellow guest, suddenly disappears into thin air on the same night that the Irish Mail is held up. Suspecting a link, Scotland Yard descends upon Bertram's Hotel.

Miss Marple's last case, *Nemesis*, published in 1971, is surely the most macabre and somber of all her adventures. Yet it is told with an air of detachment and light-heartedness perhaps reserved for the very elderly—not surprising when one considers that Agatha Christie was herself in her eightieth year when she wrote it. In this book Miss Marple ends her recorded life as a detective with great style and on a triumphant note of pleasures yet to come.

In the opening chapters of *Nemesis*, Miss Marple, leading a tottery knitting life in St. Mary Mead, receives a letter from Messrs. Broadribb and Schuster, Solicitors and Notaries Public, inviting her to visit them in London to discuss a matter that may be to her advantage. On the appointed day an astonishing proposal is put to her under the terms of the will of their recently deceased client, her old ally, Jason Rafiel: to undertake, for the sum of twenty thousand pounds, the investigation of an unspecified crime. A letter from Mr. Rafiel is produced:

> You, my dear, if I may call you that, have a natural *flair* for justice, and that has led to your having a natural *flair* for crime. I want you to investigate a certain crime. I have ordered a certain sum to be placed so that if you accept this request and as a result of your investigation this crime is properly elucidated, the money will become yours absolutely. I have set aside a year for you to engage on this mission.

Miss Marple accepts. "She's going to take it on, is she?" says Mr. Schuster to Mr. Broadribb with a whistle. "Sporting old bean." Before long she receives from a London travel agency the particulars of a two to three weeks' bus tour booked for her by Mr. Rafiel before his death. "You're a bit old, you know, to do this sort of thing," remonstrates her cheerful young housekeeper, Cherry Baker, but Miss Marple packs her bags and sets off upon her enterprise armed with guide books, itineraries, and a list of her fellow passengers.

Surely there has seldom been as eventful a trip as that which follows for the participants of Tour No. 37 of the Famous Houses and Gardens of Great Britain, particularly for passenger number 19, who not only has to follow the instructions of her tour guide but also those of Mr. Rafiel, periodically delivered from beyond the grave. Encountered along the way are murder, suicide, the revelation of great tragedies, and even an attempt on Miss Marple's life, but in the end—just as Jason Rafiel knew it would when he hired Miss Marple as his Nemesis—justice triumphs.

The wrapping up of the case—Miss Marple explaining her conclusions to some very senior people indeed—is impressive. But even greater fun is Miss Marple's collecting her twenty thousand pounds. Visions of her favorite charities, a whole partridge to herself, *marrons glacés*, a visit to the opera dance before her eyes. Asks Mr. Broadribb:

> "You have a deposit account, I expect. We will place it in your deposit account?"
>
> "Certainly not," said Miss Marple. "Put it into my current account". . .
>
> . . . Mr. Schuster, who was a man of more imagination than Mr. Broadribb, had a vague impression of a young and pretty girl shaking hands with the vicar at a garden party in the country.

Seven

The Essential Miss Marple

So charming, so innocent, such a fluffy and pink
and white old lady.

—*A Pocket Full of Rye*

What did Miss Marple look like? What sort of
person was she? What kind of things did she
do and say?

To begin with, she was not the sensible, tweedy person
or the jolly blunderer masquerading under the name of
Marple that many of us have seen in movies and on the
stage. Some of her best friends were like that, but not
Miss Marple. At the same time it must be admitted that
she was something of a chameleon—and an actress. If
it seemed appropriate and advantageous to dither and
flutter, no one could excel her; if the situation called for

a soothing confidant, no one could be more placid and discreet.

There seems to have been a bit of confusion about her looks, particularly in her earlier—though always elderly—days. As we have seen, the old Victorian lady of the Tuesday Night Club days and the other early short stories who sat by the hearth in a long black dress, with lace mittens on her hands and a lace cap on her piled-up snowy hair, evolved into a more contemporary and somewhat younger Miss Marple of about sixty who then proceeded, over the next forty years or so, to reach the age of about eighty. It is this Miss Marple who is the most familiar to us, and during this long period of her life two adjectives are most frequently used to describe her: frail and fluffy. Here are two typical examples:

> She had a very fine Shetland shawl thrown over her head and shoulders, and was looking rather old and frail. She came in full of little fluttering remarks.
>
> —*The Murder at the Vicarage* (1930)

> She sat there, upright as was her habit. She wore a light tweed suit, a string of pearls and a small velvet toque. To himself Mr. Broadribb was saying, "The Provincial Lady. A good type. Fluffy old girl. May be scatty—may not. . . . Somebody's aunt, perhaps, up from the country?"
>
> —*Nemesis* (1971)

Her hair was usually described as white, occasionally gray, her face as pink and crinkled, and her teeth as ladylike. She was tall and thin and had very pretty china-blue eyes, which could look innocent or shrewd depending on one's point of view. Her general expression was usually described as sweet, "with her head a little on one side looking like an amiable cockatoo," but this could change when she was on the trail of someone evil. Inspector Craddock noticed, in *A Murder Is Announced*, "the grimness of her lips and the severe frosty light in those usually gentle blue eyes."

Her clothes were ladylike and dowdy. There is the occasional mention of gray crepe or gray lace for evening, but for the most part they are described—like her knitting—as fleecy. A typical outing saw her at Dillmouth on the esplanade, "nicely wrapped up in a thick fleecy coat and well wound round with scarves." On her feet, at home in St. Mary Mead, she wore stout walking shoes for errands, but for her holiday in the Caribbean she purchased some neat sandals and a pair of plimsolls, "not perhaps very elegant, but admirably suited to this climate and comfortable and roomy for the feet." Again at home, she liked to wear a hat and gloves for marketing, carry an umbrella (just in case), a colorful shopping basket of foreign extraction, and a handbag. In it, one might have found "a handkerchief, an engagement book, an old-fashioned leather purse, two shillings, three pennies, and a striped piece of peppermint rock." The only mention of jewelry is a string of pearls and a "pale blue enamel watch that she wore pinned to one side of her dress."

In discussing someone as old—as perpetually old—as Miss Marple, it is surely obligatory to touch on the matter of her health. "How are you today, Miss Marple?" must have been a question asked thousands of times over the course of her long career, and anyone really pursuing the subject would have heard, first of all, about her rheumatism. Her "knee, as she would have put it to herself, was always with her"; so were her stiff fingers, which sometimes hampered her knitting; so was her stiff neck, which often made it difficult for her to look over her shoulder (a fact that considerably delayed the unmasking of the murderer in A Caribbean Mystery). From time to time she attempted to do something about these aches and pains by visiting health spas, as in "A Christmas Tragedy" and A Murder Is Announced ("Beastly places— absolutely beastly!" Colonel Bantry considered them. "Got to get up early and drink filthy-tasting water"). Generally, though, she put up with them with good grace, except in the matter of gardening. Dr. Haydock's decree in later years of "No stooping, no digging, no planting— at most a little light pruning" was obeyed with the greatest reluctance.

She was also prone to attacks of bronchitis and pneumonia, with two invariable results: the kind intervention of her nephew Raymond with an offer of a housekeeper or a holiday and, shortly thereafter, the opening chapter of a promising new murder. The latter was always Miss Marple's best medicine.

Her eyesight had its ups and downs. In her earliest recorded case, "The Thumbmark of St. Peter," it led to her solving a murder:

"I don't know anything about medicine, of course," said Miss Marple, "but I did happen to know this, that when my eyesight was failing, the doctor ordered me drops with atropine sulphate in them. I went straight upstairs to old Mr. Denman's room. I didn't beat about the bush.

'Mr. Denman,' I said, 'I know everything . . .' "

Nevertheless, many years later in *Murder with Mirrors*, we are told that "her long distance sight was good (as many of her neighbors knew to their cost in the village of St. Mary Mead)," but in *The Mirror Crack'd*, ten years after that, "even her new spectacles didn't seem to do any good," despite the luxurious waiting rooms and high fees of the oculists. She was forced to resort to a magnifying glass to decipher the small print of movie magazines while collecting background information during the Gossington Hall murders. Yet in her very next adventure, *A Caribbean Mystery*, nothing on the landscape or in her knitting escaped her; in *At Bertram's Hotel* we are told "Miss Marple had remarkable eyesight for her age." Perhaps this mystery *is* best left to the oculists.

As the years went by she became slightly deaf. "People do not seem to me to enunciate their words as clearly as they used to do," she remarked in *What Mrs. McGillicuddy Saw!*, but to compensate we are told in *A Caribbean Mystery* that her blood pressure was very good for her age.

As to medicines, she believed in the old-fashioned remedies: Easton's Syrup, linseed poultices, cobwebs on a cut, camphorated oil for a cough, a glass of cowslip wine followed by camomile tea for overexcitement, hot-water bottles and very sweet tea for shock. "I don't know anything about drugs—nasty, dangerous things I call them. I have got an old recipe of my grandmother's for tansy tea that is worth any amount of your drugs," but if she had to have a prescription she preferred it in a bottle reminiscent of the "mixtures" of her youth rather than pills.

She also took a dim view of doctors:

> "I have had too much experience of life to believe in the infallibility of doctors. Some of them are clever men and some of them are not, and half the time the best of them don't know what is the matter with you."

The shining exception to all this was her own Dr. Haydock, who was one of her greatest friends and a very wise man. "For a woman of your age," he once told her, "and in spite of that misleading frail appearance, you're in remarkably good fettle." *He* knew what was her best tonic.

When she was very elderly indeed, Miss Marple had to endure a number of the indignities of extreme old age: forgetfulness, the occasional fall, the insistence of her doctor and relatives that she never be alone. But—gerontologists take note—none of these annoyances prevented her from pursuing her great interest in life, the solving of murders. What she did resent very much was the "calm assumption that everyone of advanced years was liable to die at any minute."

Thus Miss Marple's appearance and health. What was she like as a person?

"Raymond always says (only quite kindly, because he is the kindest of nephews) I am hopelessly Victorian," she once mused. She loved to quote Raymond, and opinions of his are scattered throughout her cases. "As I've told you, I've got a very suspicious mind. My nephew Raymond tells me, in fun, of course—that I have a mind like a sink. He says that most Victorians have." Raymond was right. If there was one characteristic of Miss Marple's that emerged over and over again, it was that she always believed the worst. "It really is very dangerous to believe people," she once said, "*I* never have for years," which goes a long way toward explaining why she was such a superb detective. "Not a nice trait," she once confessed, "but so often justified by subsequent events."

She was also extremely inquisitive: "Curiosity, or what she preferred herself to call 'taking an interest' in other people's affairs, was undoubtedly one of Miss Marple's characteristics." "People call her a scandalmonger," Mrs. Bantry once declared, "but she isn't really." It was just Miss Marple's way—again, of the good detective—of finding out the facts. "*How often is tittle tattle*, as you call it, *true!*" was how she rationalized this characteristic; and, indeed, without her genius for sifting through the flotsam of conversations and confidences she so cleverly encouraged over tea, over knitting, over canvassing for the church, what would have happened to law and order in a number of English villages? But like the true professional that she was, she also knew how to keep her mouth shut. It is always amazing, at the end of a case, how much Miss Marple knew all along and never told anyone, including close friends, relatives, the clergy, and Scotland Yard. Her old friend Carrie Louise was right when she told her, "You could always keep a secret, Jane."

She could also tell lies. "Miss Marple had been brought up to have a proper regard for truth and was indeed by nature a very truthful person. But on certain occasions, when she considered it her duty so to do, she could tell lies with a really astonishing verisimilitude." Who, after all, could disbelieve a fluffy old lady with china-blue eyes and a "gentle, soft voice"? Perhaps Dr. Haydock, when she was feigning illness as a cover, but scarcely anyone else. Certainly not the Crackenthorpe family of Rutherford Hall in *What Mrs. McGillicuddy Saw!*, led to believe that the boring old lady who kept turning up for tea was their housekeeper's aunt, or the kindly postmistress in *Nemesis*, maneuvered into revealing the address of someone else's parcel, or the extremely dangerous murderer of *A Murder Is Announced*, tricked into believing that a voice in a broom cupboard belonged to the dead.

Many of these fibs and subterfuges depended upon Miss Marple's skill as an actress and mimic. She was never better at concealing her real purpose than when she was fluttering—"fluttering a little in the restless manner that she adopted when slightly flustered. Or at any rate, when she was seeming to be slightly flustered." On such occasions—woolly and twittering, wending her way apologetically to the point while jumping from rheumatism to nephews to knitting patterns—she was almost always dangerous. One's attention could wander, one's guard could go down and, suddenly, gone would be the alibi, snap would go the trap. Interestingly enough, when a situation did not call for fluttering, Miss Marple could speak very precisely, almost pedantically. Her last case, *Nemesis*, provides some examples of this: "Is there no more definite elucidation of any kind?" she asks the solicitor, Mr. Broadribb, and remarks, in the same conversation, "I am not at all cognizant of financial matters myself." It is in the same book, however, that she resorts to a bit of slang: "With bells on" and "done me very proud!" Of course, she never *swore*.

Another interesting side to Miss Marple's character was her outlook on gentlemen. " 'Gentlemen,' she said, with her old maid's way of referring to the opposite sex as though it were a species of wild animal," and she had a whole set of formulae forever on hand to try to explain them. "Gentlemen always make such excellent memoranda." "Gentlemen, she knew, did not like to be put right in their facts." "Gentlemen are so clever at arranging things." "Gentlemen, when they've had a disappointment want something stronger than tea." Gentlemen "are frequently not so levelheaded as they seem." She appreciated good looks in a man, telling Inspector Craddock in *What Mrs. McGillicuddy Saw!* that he was better-looking than ever, and later in the same case smiling up at Alfred Crackenthorpe "with the approval she always showed towards a good-looking man." Was she a feminist? Apparently not, which is a pity, since she was such an endearing example of an independent woman competently running her own life. She did once say, however, "What I do realize is that women must stick together—one should, in an emergency, stand by one's own sex."

This permissible use of the word "sex" is one of the few times Miss Marple uttered this word until the latter years of her career. It simply was not done. Said the rambling Major Palgrave in *A Caribbean Mystery*:

> "I could tell you a lot more. Some of the things, of course, not fit for a lady's ears—"
> With the ease of long practice, Miss Marple dropped her eyelids in a fluttery fashion, and Major Palgrave continued his bowdlerised version of tribal customs.

She and Miss Hartnell and Miss Wetherby liked to talk about it, though.

> Miss Wetherby said tersely, "No nice girl would do it," and shut her thin lips disapprovingly.
> "Do what?" I inquired.
> "Be a secretary to an unmarried man," said Miss Wetherby in a horrified tone.
> "Oh, my dear," said Miss Marple. "I think married ones are the worst. Remember poor Mollie Carter."

And she once surprised Sir Henry Clithering into "a peculiar sort of cough" when, speaking of the language of flowers, the actress Jane Helier said dreamily, "A man used to send me purple orchids every night to the theater" and Miss Marple replied brightly, " 'I Await Your Favors'—that's what that means."

When she was a very old lady, however, Miss Marple spoke much more frankly about sex:

"Sex" as a word had not been mentioned in Miss Marple's young days, but there had been plenty of it—not talked about so much—but enjoyed far more than nowadays, or so it seemed to her. Though usually labelled Sin, she couldn't help feeling that that was preferable to what it seemed nowadays—a kind of Duty.

And she was able to briskly label things that went on in St. Mary Mead that she and Miss Hartnell and Miss Wetherby had only hinted at years before:

Plenty of sex, natural and unnatural. Rape, incest, perversion of all kinds (Some kinds, indeed, that even the clever young men from Oxford who wrote books didn't seem to have heard about).

She was, of course, extremely intelligent, and she ordered her thoughts, as the last chapters of all her books testify, with a competence bordering on genius. "Miss Marple is not the type of elderly lady who makes mistakes," wrote the Reverend Leonard Clement. "She has got an uncanny knack of being always right." Nothing escaped her, and she rarely made a mistake. If she did, she had the ability to jettison all her preconceived ideas and theories in a flash and start afresh. She also possessed a very shrewd common sense. "What I like about you," the learned Professor Wanstead told her in *Nemesis,* "is your delightfully practical mind." She was also, in the words of Lucy Eyelesbarrow, "eminently sane."

Was she a snob? Certainly not in the arrogant sense, but as a "provincial gentlewoman" she had very definite opinions on one's proper station in life—depending on who one was—and an unerring eye for anyone stepping out of line. Servants were expected to be deferential, police officers polite, and people of what she delicately called "our own class of life" to be ladies and gentlemen. As for foreigners, one never really *knew*.

A fascinating conversation between Miss Marple and Sir Henry Clithering took place in *The Body in the Library*:

"A well-bred girl," continued Miss Marple, warming to her subject, "is always very particular to wear the right clothes for the right occasion. I mean, however hot the day was, a well-bred girl would never turn up at a point-to-point in a silk flowered frock."

"And the correct wear to meet a lover?" demanded Sir Henry.

"If she were meeting him inside the hotel or somewhere where evening dress was worn, she'd wear her best evening frock, of course, but outside she'd feel she'd look ridiculous in evening dress and she'd wear her most attractive sports wear."

"Granted, Fashion Queen, but the girl Ruby—"

Miss Marple said, "Ruby, of course, wasn't—well, to put it bluntly, Ruby wasn't a lady. She belonged to the class that wear their best clothes, however unsuitable to the occasion."

In *A Pocket Full of Rye* a more mellow conversation occurred between Miss Marple and young Pat Fortescue, recently married into the rich and vulgar Fortescue family. "A background of shabby chintz and horses and dogs, Miss Marple felt vaguely, would have been much more suitable than this richly furnished interior décor." She warmed to Pat immediately and later, over knitting, found an occasion to say:

"If I might venture to advise, if anything ever—goes wrong in your life—I think the happiest thing for you would be to go back to where you were happy as a child. Go back to Ireland, my dear. Horses and dogs. All that."

"All that" was very important to Miss Marple.

Was she religious? A well-brought-up Anglican, she certainly attended church regularly and undertook her share of parish duties, but, ladylike Victorian that she was, she rarely talked about God (or politics, either, for that matter). The most important creed in her life was simply to do one's duty. But she did say once: "Now, I dare say you modern young people will laugh, but when I am in really bad trouble I always say a little prayer to myself—anywhere, when I am walking along the street, or at a bazaar. And I always get an answer." She liked to begin and end her day with a quiet bit of religious reading, and when she was a very old lady she firmly declared, "I believe in eternal life."

She also believed very strongly in justice of the old-fashioned kind. Though trained to suppress strong emotions, she could become very angry—and tears would come to her eyes—with pity for a hapless victim and "anger against a heartless killer." She was very much opposed to the abolition of capital punishment and did indeed regard herself, in a modest way, as an avenger or nemesis. To her, evil was evil. "If you expect me to feel sympathy, regret, urge an unhappy childhood, blame bad environment . . . I do not feel inclined so to do," she once said of a young murderer.

Finally, despite her fragile appearance, it should not

be forgotten that Miss Marple was very brave. In several instances she saved people's lives, as in *Sleeping Murder* when she rescued a victim from strangling by deftly squirting a jet of soapy water into the killer's eyes. On other occasions, to catch a criminal, she set herself as bait for a trap. A good example of this is in *Nemesis*, where, faced with a three-time murderer about to kill *her*, we find her "sitting up in bed with a pink fluffy shawl round her neck and a perfectly placid face, twittering away and talking like an elderly school marm."

She was, as Jason Rafiel remarked in his posthumous letter, tough. Inspector Craddock once put it this way: "Miss Marple can contemplate murder and sudden death and indeed crime of all kinds with the utmost equanimity." Walter Hudd, a young American in *Murder with Mirrors*, said much the same thing:

> "Don't know what it is about you—you're English right enough, really English—but in the durndest way you remind me of my Aunt Betsy back home."
>
> "Now that's very nice."
>
> "A lot of sense she had," Wally continued reflectively. "Looked as frail as though you could snap her in two, but actually she was tough—yes, sir, I'll say she was tough."

Eight

A Visit to Miss Marple

We were admitted by a very diminutive maid
and shown into a small drawing-room.
　　—Rev. Leonard Clement, *The Murder at
　　　　　　　　　　　　　　the Vicarage*

If you look very hard at the plan of St. Mary Mead
provided in *The Murder at the Vicarage* and in the first
chapter of this book, you will see the roof of Miss
Marple's house in a "little nest of Queen Anne and Georgian houses, of which hers was one." It sits squarely in
the middle of an elongated garden facing the shops and
small houses of the High Street. Her neighbor to the left
was Dr. Haydock, to the right Miss Hartnell. Both these
houses appear to be more elaborate than Miss Marple's,
which is sometimes referred to as an "old-world cottage."
The back of her property adjoins the vicarage garden and

faces onto a small lane. It all looks very charming and indeed, by all reports, it was. If you had come as an overnight guest, walking up the neat brick path from the street to the front door, what would you have found inside?

If you had arrived in the earlier days, you would have been admitted by one of a succession of Miss Marple's neatly uniformed maids—Emily, or Gwen, or perhaps even Faithful Florence. If you had arrived in the later years, you would have been met by a housekeeper: the wonderful Lucy Eyelesbarrow, for example, or the awful Miss Knight. But let us imagine that it is the earlier days, and that it is Emily who has answered the door and led you across a hall, past a table where the calling cards and letters are put, past a row of pegs and a stand for Miss Marple's walking stick, and into Miss Marple's pretty, old-fashioned drawing room. If you had been a member of the Tuesday Night Club, you would have seen a room that was "an old one with broad black beams across the ceiling and it was furnished with good old furniture that belonged to it." If you had been Colonel Melchett, you would have looked around and remarked to your companion, "A bit crowded . . . But plenty of good stuff. A lady's room, eh, Clement?" If you had been Mr. Petherick, Miss Marple's lawyer, you might not have been shown into the drawing room at all but into the dining room instead, as "in early spring I think it is so wasteful to have two fires going."

Three of the drawing room chairs were favorites of Miss Marple's: the chair by the window, the big grandfather chair by the hearth, and, in later years, "a specially purchased, upright armchair which catered to the demands of her rheumatic back." There was a bookcase that held reference books, including a medical book that helped Miss Marple solve a murder in *The Mirror Crack'd;* two lamps; a corner cupboard, which contained old Waterford glasses; and another cupboard, which contained bottles. On the mantelpiece were lusters, and underfoot was probably a good carpet because Miss Marple had something of an eye for them, noting in the Old Manor House in *Nemesis* that the carpet was probably Irish, "possibly a Limerick Aubusson type." Also in the drawing room was a telephone. In those days Miss Marple's number was three five.

Having sat down in the drawing room, you would almost certainly have been offered something to drink, and, surprisingly, it was rarely tea. The cupboard with the bottles held quite a collection: a decanter of sherry, cherry brandy made from "a receipt of my grandmother's," cowslip wine, damson gin, whiskey, and a siphon of soda water for the gentlemen. In the matter of food and drink, Miss Marple was ruthlessly sexist.

If you had arrived in the early evening, it would now be time for dinner. One gets the impression that food was not of much interest in Miss Marple's life, which was perhaps why she was so nice and thin. She considered Mrs. Beeton "a wonderful book but terribly expensive; most of the recipes begin, 'Take a quart of cream and a dozen eggs.' " If you were a male guest, however, dinner would almost certainly have included meat ("Gentlemen require such a lot of meat, do they not?") and you would no doubt have eaten it off Miss Marple's old Worcester china. In the dining room was another corner cupboard, which probably held Miss Marple's plate and her King Charles tankard.

After dinner you and your hostess would have returned to the drawing room for more conversation before the fire, and Miss Marple, sitting in the big grandfather chair, would have brought out her knitting: a comforter for old Mrs. Hay, or a coat for the offspring of one of her former maids ("I always say young mothers can't have too many matinée coats for their babies"), or a wedding present for her young friends in Lymstock, Megan Hunter and Jerry Burton ("That fluffy woolly thing that we didn't know what it's for from Miss Marple"), or, in later years, a pullover for her great-nephew David West.

Her brows might have puckered a little as she counted the stitches. She might have interrupted the conversation from time to time ("I must just count this row. The decreasing is a little awkward. One, two, three, four, five, and then three purl"). Or, if things became animated, she might even have shaken a knitting needle at you ("No legal quibbles, now," she once admonished Mr. Petherick). But whatever you said—particularly if it was something even remotely connected with the current murder—would be carefully taken in, weighed, and stored away for possible future use. "One has a lot of opportunities," she once said, "doing one's needlework round the fire."

In Miss Marple's home, bedtime came well before midnight. As a guest, you would have been led up a staircase "of the old-fashioned kind which turned in a sharp corner in the middle" and to a bedroom containing a dressing table swathed modestly in chintz to conceal its legs, and a bed made up with Miss Marple's best monogrammed frilled sheets, well aired earlier in the day by Emily. Downstairs, behind you, the front door would have been securely locked against the night with a brass hook and eye.

At breakfast the next morning, if you were a woman, the conversation might have turned to domestic matters. "Slugs, you know—and the difficulty of getting linen properly darned—and not being able to get sugar candy for making my damson gin." If you had appeared particularly interested you might have been given a tour behind the scenes: the kitchen, the pantry where the washing up was done, and, in a burst of confidence, the linen closet. Ah, that linen closet! Surely Miss Marple's linen closet was one of the passions of her life, and keeping it well stocked was the reason for almost all her recorded expeditions to London:

> Miss Marple had a very enjoyable time at Robinson & Cleaver's. Besides purchasing expensive but delicious sheets—she loved linen sheets with their texture and their coolness—she also indulged in a purchase of good quality red-bordered glass-cloths. Really the difficulty in getting proper glass-cloths nowadays!

And now it would have been time for a turn around the garden, the famous garden "so admirably placed to see all that was going on in St. Mary Mead." Rev. Leonard Clement called it the "danger point." On the morning of your visit, however, let us suppose that you and your hostess have been spared the sight of any distractions such as scandal or murder and would simply have concentrated on the garden itself, which must have been a lovely place, full of the old-fashioned flowers Miss Marple loved best: hollyhocks, larkspurs, Canterbury Bells, snapdragons, sweetpeas, and roses. She would no doubt have pointed out to you her Japanese gardens as well, for which a murderer once brought the wrong sort of stone. "And that put me on the right track!" she might have exclaimed, pulling up a nasty piece of bindwood. It would have soon become clear that Miss Marple looked at gardens in "either a mood of admiration or a mood of criticism," and she might, that morning, have indulged in a few reminiscences about other gardens encountered during her adventures. Most of them were pretty dreadful: the garden at Yewtree Lodge in *A Pocket Full of Rye*, for example ("The gardens were highly artificial—all laid out in rose beds and pergolas and pools"); the weeds and "large gloomy clumps of rhododendrons" at Rutherford Hall in *What Mrs. McGillicuddy Saw!*; the overgrown rockeries of "Greenshaw's Folly" ("Alyssum, saxifrage, cystis, thimble campanula . . . Yes, that's all the proof I need"); or the very strange things that were discovered in the neglected gardens at Hillside in *Sleeping Murder* and the Old Manor House in *Nemesis*.

By this time you would have arrived at the back of Miss Marple's own trim house to find nothing more threatening than a neat jasmine hedge where, she might have told you with a little spinsterish cough, dear Raymond had once courted the artist Joyce Lemprière, and Annie, a former maid, had received a proposal of marriage from the milkman.

After admiring the old stables and the greenhouse (omitted on the map) and noticing that the vegetable garden was very small ("I like flowers best. Don't care so much for vegetables"), you would then have been led back into the house through the French window of the drawing room for a glass of sherry, perhaps, and an early lunch while waiting for Inch to arrive to drive you to the 12:15 train. After your departure, if you had been a smoker, Miss Marple would have immediately set about opening the windows and shaking out the curtains.

Upon returning home, I am sure you would have sat down at once to write Miss Marple a letter and send her a box of *marrons glacés* to an address apparently adequate:

> Miss Jane Marple
> St. Mary Mead
> Much Benham

Nine

Miss Marple at Home

I don't know why you should assume that I think of murder *all* the time.

—*The Mirror Crack'd*

When at home in St. Mary Mead and not occupied with a visitor or a murderer, how did Miss Marple spend her time? "Inertia does not suit me," she once declared, and it will come as no surprise to learn that her days were passed in a most orderly fashion.

"Miss Marple awoke early because she always woke early." Upon waking she immediately pulled back her curtains, got back into bed, picked up a small book of devotions and "read as usual the page and a half allotted to the day." This done, she sometimes picked up her knitting—just to give her rheumatic fingers a head start—

and awaited the arrival of her current maid or house-keeper with her breakfast tray, for Miss Marple, when alone, loved to eat breakfast in bed. Tea, an egg (boiled three and three-quarter minutes), toast, butter, and honey, or sometimes herrings, were followed by the first post of the day and a newspaper. Her mail she opened "neatly with the paper knife she always kept handy on her tray"— letters first, then bills and receipts—and her newspaper was the *Daily Newsgiver*:

> . . . men's tailoring, women's dress, female heart-throbs, competitions for children, and complaining letters from women . . . had managed pretty well to shove any real news off any part of it but the front page, or to some obscure corner where it was impossible to find it.

Miss Marple called it "The Daily All-sorts."

Once dressed, telephoning was next on the agenda. "Nine o'clock to nine-thirty was the recognized time for the village to make friendly calls to neighbors. Plans for the day, invitations, and so on, were always issued then." Occasionally the telephone rang earlier—Dolly Bantry phoned twice over the years to announce, before eight o'clock in the morning, that bodies had been discovered at Gossington Hall, and "the butcher had been known to ring up just before nine if some crisis in the meat trade had occurred"—but these were the exceptions.

Household matters were then dealt with. There were various deliveries during the morning—the bread, the meat, the fish brought by young Fred—and no doubt conversations in the kitchen on the meals for the day, the state of the current wine making, and the progress of spring cleaning.

This done, if the weather was fine, Miss Marple would almost certainly spend some time in the garden, either supervising the jobbing gardener, if that was his day, or doing some snipping or pruning herself, for gardening was "the source of great pleasure and also a great deal of hard work to Miss Marple for many, many years." And sometime in the course of the morning there would be a visit to the High Street for shopping, for business, to see and be seen, for the High Street was the nursery.of most of the news in St. Mary Mead. Bits and variations of it surfaced elsewhere during the day—with the deliveries, on the telephone, at afternoon tea—but nothing equaled going there oneself and doing the rounds of the Fish Shop, to have a word with the young assistant whom one suspected of juggling one's accounts; to the chemist's, with a sidelong glance at the young lady who worked in Mr. Badger's cosmetics section; to Barnes, the grocer's, reassuringly unchanged over the years; and to the wool shop for a leisurely discussion of patterns and relatives.

After luncheon, in the later years, Miss Marple liked to nap for twenty minutes in her upright armchair in the drawing room and then read her second newspaper of the day, *The Times:*

> The maddening thing about *The Times* was that you couldn't find anything any more. . . . Two pages were suddenly devoted to Capri with illustrations. Sport appeared with far more prominence than it ever had in the old days. Court news and obituaries were a little more

faithful to routine. The births, marriages and deaths which had at one time occupied Miss Marple's attention first of all owing to their prominent position had migrated to a different part of *The Times*, though of late, Miss Marple noted, they had come almost permanently to rest on the back page.

She might, if there was time, do the crossword (in *What Mrs. McGillicuddy Saw!* it helped her solve a series of murders), and then followed the major activities of the afternoon. If one had called upon Miss Marple at, say, ten minutes past three, like Mr. Spenlow in "Tape-Measure Murder," one would probably have been told she was "not at 'ome," for this was the time of day for parish activities and, you may depend upon it, she was never late. "Her clock keeps time to the minute, and she herself is rigidly punctual on every occasion," wrote the Vicar. As we have seen, the parish activities were many, varied, and designed to do good: a meeting of the Women's Institute, perhaps, or the Orphanage Committee, or the organization of a sale of work. "She's frivolous, like all Church of England people," the puritanical old Miss Ramsbottom in *A Pocket Full of Rye* declared of Miss Marple, "but she knows how to run a charity in a sensible way." Not all these events were as dull as one might suppose. Miss Marple once recalled a very lively meeting for Armenian Relief when an elderly clergyman took off all his clothes. "They telephoned his wife and she came along at once and took him home in a cab, wrapped in a blanket."

This would certainly be meat for the next event, "tea

and scandal at four-thirty" with Miss Hartnell and Miss Wetherby. Once the current scandals were dealt with in the worst possible light, the conversation might turn to health, as it did with the old ladies in *Nemesis*:

> They discussed happily arthritis, rheumatism, diets, new doctors, remedies both professional, patent, and reminiscences of old wives' treatments which had had success where all else failed.

Between tea (Miss Marple liked her tea clear and preferred scones and butter to cake) and "her frugal evening meal," she would often be seen at work in her garden or indulging in a little birdwatching. Whether in pursuit of weeds or a double-crested wren, "Miss Marple always sees everything. Gardening is as good as a smoke screen, and the habit of observing birds through powerful glasses can always be turned to account." Again the Vicar. And how did he know all this? one is prompted to ask.

But if the weather was not fine, or if it was winter, and if there was nothing else particularly to do, Miss Marple might perhaps retire to her drawing room to read for an hour or so before supper. She was not an avid reader of books, but she did take up the occasional novel: a Mark Twain, for example, or *Three Men in a Boat*, or Richard Hughes's *A High Wind in Jamaica*, and of course there was always her own dear Raymond's latest novel to read, though sometimes, it must be confessed, his aunt found this a struggle: "Raymond writes those very modern books all about rather unpleasant young men and women." In the matter of her reading, her nephew was always trying to keep her up to date. Not only did he send her his own novels but also those of his contemporaries, stark, sex-ridden, "all about such unpleasant people, doing such very odd things and not, apparently, even enjoying them."

"I have never read books on criminology," Miss Marple once said, but she did occasionally resort to whodunits for inspiration. "I have been reading a lot of American detective stories from the library lately," she confided to the Vicar, "hoping to find them helpful." She also worked her way through Dashiell Hammett's stories, on Raymond's recommendation, as he considered them "at the top of the tree in what is called the 'tough' style of literature." Another type of literature she once pursued was movie magazines. In *The Mirror Crack'd,* in order to better understand the new tenants of Gossington Hall, she borrowed a huge stack from Mrs. Jameson, the hairdresser, and was soon deep in *Movie News* and *Amongst the Stars.* "Really very interesting," she reported. They remind "one so much of so many things."

While reading, Miss Marple sometimes liked to crochet, her eyes on her book while her fingers proceeded "correctly through their appointed movements." Perhaps if she became very engrossed (with *Film Life?*), or if she had had a very tiring afternoon, she might stay by the fire and have her evening meal brought to her on a tray. Occasionally she might go out for dinner, or one of her neighbors might drop in for a chat, but generally the evening was devoted to her own affairs: more knitting, more reading, and the odd telephone call, though "it was considered bad form to ring up after nine-thirty at night." This was probably also the time Miss Marple wrote letters in a "spiky and spidery and heavily underlined" handwriting (which Sir Henry Clithering found neat and old-fashioned) and did her accounts.

Miss Marple had a limited income and was very careful with her money. "Money," she once said, "can do a lot to ease one's path in life." Beware the shop assistant who overcharged her, or the hotel clerk, as in *A Murder Is Announced*, who tried to alter a check. "I was quite the wrong person," she said smugly of that event. "Women have a lot of sense, you know, when it comes to money matters." Unfortunately she went on to add "not high finance, of course. No woman can hope to understand *that*, my dear father said."

In 1948, also in *A Murder Is Announced*, we get a glimpse of her postwar budget: twenty pounds for the monthly wages and the bills and seven pounds for personal expenditures. "It used to be five, but everything has gone up so." It is clear that Miss Marple's circumstances would have become straitened indeed as the years went by had it not been for her generous nephew:

> . . . she was not in urgent need of money. She had her dear and affectionate nephew who, if she was in straits for money of any kind, if she needed repairs to her house or a visit to a specialist or special treats, dear Raymond would always provide them.

Of course she would never have dreamed of charging money for all the detective work she did, which ladylike attitude must have caused her to be considerably out of pocket at times, what with all those train journeys and staying in lodgings to be near the scenes of crimes. In *What Mrs. McGillicuddy Saw!*, for example, she persuaded Mrs. McGillicuddy to join her in retracing the journey in which she had seen a woman being strangled on a train: "*I*, of course, would pay the *fares*." And later we find her, in the interests of planting Lucy Eyelesbarrow as her agent inside Rutherford Hall, paying the difference between the modest salary the Crackenthorpes would offer a housekeeper and the high one that the incomparable Lucy Eyelesbarrow would expect. It is ironic that it is also in this case that Miss Marple was paid the first of the only two professional fees she was ever to receive when Inspector Craddock "solemnly drew out his notecase, extracted three pound notes, added three shillings and pushed them across the table to Miss Marple.

> "What's this, Inspector?"
> "Consultation fee. You're a consultant—on murder!"

It took Jason Rafiel, that shrewd old millionaire, to recognize Miss Marple's true worth when he offered her, from beyond the grave, twenty thousand pounds to solve a mystery.

Having completed her accounts and letters, it would then have been time to wind the clocks, lock the door, and go to bed. Miss Marple was quite capable of staying up till midnight and treading the High Street alone, as in *The Murder at the Vicarage*, if she thought it might help solve a murder, and occasionally there was a very late phone call (Raymond "had been known to ring up at the most peculiar times; once as late as ten minutes to midnight"), but as a habit she and her hot water bottle retired early to bed.

Beside it was a little table on which stood a clock, her knitting, and her morning and evening devotional books. At night Miss Marple read a few verses of Thomas à Kempis and then turned out the light. If sleep did not come immediately there was no resorting to sleeping pills. "I bet you, if you asked Miss Marple what she does if she can't sleep, she'd tell you she counted sheep going under a gate," remarked old Dr. Graham in *A Caribbean Mystery*. If she had to get up in the night to investigate strange events or make notes on a case very much on her mind, she had a dressing gown and slippers nearby and a "fluffy scarf of pale pink wool" for her head.

> Like many old people she slept lightly and had periods of wakefulness which she used for the planning of some action or actions to be carried out on the next or following days.

Thus a day in the life of Miss Marple.

Ten

Miss Marple at Large

I wonder what she's doing now, the dear old
thing. Sitting in the sun on the front?
—Gwenda Reed, *Sleeping Murder*

There was a fiction in Miss Marple's life, encouraged by her, that she seldom stirred from home. "My outlook, I'm afraid, is a very petty one," she once said. "I hardly ever go out of St. Mary Mead." This was quite untrue. As a child she visited Paris with her mother and grandmother, and as a young girl she spent some time at a finishing school in Florence. Whether there were any other expeditions to the Continent we do not know, but in her later years as a detective she seemed forever to be away from home on holidays where murders happened to occur at the same time, away from home pretending to be on holiday because news of an interesting murder had aroused her curiosity, or actually summoned from home by relatives or friends because a murderer was at large.

When going away Miss Marple packed carefully and had "her own ways of folding things." Into her "aged but good quality" suitcase went her clothes, her devotional books, her traveling clock, her embroidered knitting bag, and a woolly shawl. A few last-minute instructions to the maid (in the early days she would have been put on board wages), and Miss Marple was ready, a nemesis off on a train.

In the first of these recorded journeys, "The Thumbmark of St. Peter," she traveled to an unnamed town to rescue her trying niece, Mabel Denman, from suspicion of poisoning her husband. Miss Marple reconnoitering this town is a great deal of fun. Also in the early days was the Christmas she spent at Keston Spa Hydro for her rheumatism. Appropriately named "A Christmas Tragedy," this holiday saw Miss Marple solve a most unpleasant hotel murder; whether or not she and her fellow guests managed to have a merry Christmas is another question. In a third early short story, "Strange Jest," Miss Marple was persuaded to search for a missing inheritance at the country home of two anxious young friends of the actress Jane Helier.

Off she went again in *The Body in the Library* with Dolly Bantry to stay in the Majestic Hotel in Danemouth to rest Dolly's nerves, and in *The Moving Finger* she was summoned to Lymstock by Mrs. Dane Calthrop, the Vicar's wife, to deal with the horrors suddenly overtaking that peaceful village. In *Sleeping Murder* she was particularly peripatetic. First discovered visiting the Wests in London, she was then off to stay with friends in the north of England, back to London to discuss someone's "hallucinations" over tea, home briefly to St. Mary Mead to persuade Dr. Haydock to send her away for her "health," and then on to Dillmouth to stay in lodgings by the sea.

Her first postwar holiday, recorded in *A Murder Is Announced*, was to the Royal Spa Hotel in Medenham Wells, a treat provided by her nephew Raymond and abruptly cut sort by enticing news of a baffling murder at nearby Chipping Cleghorn. The vicarage at Chipping Cleghorn, where Bunch Harmon lived, was Miss Marple's next port of call. A few years later in *Murder with Mirrors* she was planted by an old friend for a few weeks as a sort of poor relation/spy inside "Stonygates," a big house converted into a home for juvenile delinquents. This working holiday did nothing to improve Miss Marple's opinion of either juvenile delinquents or psychiatrists.

In *A Pocket Full of Rye* Miss Marple briskly insinuated herself into Yewtree Lodge, a mansion in London's stockbroker belt, to find out who murdered poor, silly Gladys Martin, her former maid, and left a clothes-peg clipped on her nose. A nasty case, indeed, but better times were to follow with her next trip to London, in "Sanctuary," to stay in Raymond's and Joan's studio for a fortnight while they traveled to America. The pleasant surprise of Bunch Harmon dropping in with the problem of another Chipping Cleghorn murder was only exceeded by the satisfaction of battling with her through the November sales (" 'Really a prewar-quality face towel,' gasped Miss Marple").

"Greenshaw's Folly" saw her staying for a few weeks with Raymond and Joan in their country home and solving the local mystery of who murdered nutty old Miss Greenshaw. Not long after, Miss Marple was off again, in *What Mrs. McGillicuddy Saw!*, to stay in the town of Brackhampton to be on hand to direct Lucy Eyelesbarrow's investigation of suspicious events at gloomy Rutherford Hall.

Her last three recorded holidays were the most interesting and most expensive. Arranged by Raymond, probably her first trip by airplane took her, in *A Caribbean Mystery*, to spend the winter at the Golden Palm Hotel on the Island of St. Honoré in the West Indies. And what luxury! A nice little bungalow of one's own, smiling servants, and a new dress to wear to dinner. Let others abandon themselves to light cotton prints; Miss Marple "was attired in the best traditions of the provincial gentlewomen of England—grey lace." On top of all this an interesting murder took place to dispel any possible ennui.

Much more to her taste was her holiday the following year. Was there no end to the Wests' generosity? "But it's *good* for you, Aunt Jane. Good to get away from home sometimes. It gives you new ideas, and new things to think about," argued Joan West when Miss Marple hesitated at her offer of two weeks at Bournemouth. Eastbourne, perhaps? Or Torquay? In a burst of confidence Miss Marple finally replied, "I would really like to go to

Bertram's Hotel—in London." This was a holiday she really did mind having interrupted by murder, which was perhaps why she left more of the case in *At Bertram's Hotel* to the police than was her habit. Such an opportunity for shopping! And the afternoon teas:

> Presiding over the ritual was Henry, a large and magnificent figure, a ripe fifty, avuncular, sympathetic, and with the courtly manners of that long vanished species: the perfect butler. . . . There were large crested silver trays, and Georgian silver teapots. The china, if not actually Rockingham and Davenport, looked like it.

Nemesis saw her packing "her small over-night bag [and] her new and smart suitcase" for her first paid working holiday, a leisurely coach tour of Famous Houses and Gardens of Great Britain. "I have not seen very many big and famous houses in my life," said Miss Marple, and in fact she saw more and more of murder and less and less of famous houses as the tour progressed.

Each time Miss Marple went away she did not necessarily encounter murders, though the score was high. On shorter trips, especially up to London, she sometimes had time for other things. We have seen something of her passion for shopping for linens, but it cannot be emphasized too strongly how seriously she took these missions. The bus routes that led to the great old department stores were well known to her:

> It was time to go out and enjoy the pleasures of London. She might walk as far as Piccadilly, and take a No. 9 bus to High Street, Kensington, or she might walk along to Bond Street and take a 25 bus to Marshall & Snel-

grove's or she might take a 25 the other way which as far as she remembered would land her up at the Army & Navy Stores. Passing through the swing doors she was still savouring these delights in her mind.

Though Miss Marple did know something of art—she instantly recognized a picture in Marina Gregg's hall as Bellini's "Laughing Madonna," for example, and she admired Victorian artists such as Alma-Tadema and Frederick Leighton—"it has to be regretfully noted that she did not avail herself of the wide cultural activities that would have been possible to her. She visited no picture galleries and no museums" when in London, but she did love the opera and enjoyed the theater, and she had a good eye for staging, as in *Macbeth*:

> "You know, Raymond, my dear, if *I* were ever producing this splendid play I would make the three witches *quite* different. I would have them three ordinary, normal old women. Old Scottish women. They wouldn't dance or caper. They would look at each other rather slyly and you would feel a sort of menace just behind the ordinariness of them."

She knew Barrie's plays well (" 'though I must say that when I went with an old friend of mine, General Easterly, to see Barrie's *Little Mary*'—she shook her head sadly— 'neither of us knew where to look.' "). She enjoyed a performance of *Agamemnon* at a well-known boys' school near St. Mary Mead and a performance of *The Duchess of Malfi* with Sir John Gielgud at His Majesty's Theatre in London, but modern theater was not much to her taste. A Russian play at the Witmore, to which the Wests once took her on her birthday ("absolutely the most significant piece of drama for the last twenty years") left her unmoved. "Interesting, though perhaps a little too long," she reported to the Bantrys.

She liked movies, and in *The Mirror Crack'd* we are given the impression that she was a bit of a buff. Speaking of Marina Gregg,

> "How very lovely she was," said Miss Marple with a sigh. "I always remember those early films of hers. *Bird of Passage* with that handsome Joel Roberts. And the Mary, Queen of Scots film. And of course it was very sentimental, but I *did* enjoy *Comin' Thru the Rye*."

Some of her nicest day trips over the years were invitations from Ruth Van Rydock, her old American friend from the Florence days, to lunch with her in London. Off they would go, Mrs. Van Rydock in a recent Paris creation, Miss Marple in her "dowdy black," to eat at Claridges, the Savoy, the Berkeley, or the Dorchester. Alas, we are never told what they ate (unlike many other detectives, Miss Marple did not dwell on food), but these luncheons must have made for enjoyable telling to Miss Wetherby and Miss Hartnell at tea the next day.

On at least one occasion Miss Marple went up to London to look up a marriage at Somerset House, which brings us to a curious point in her life as a sleuth. Over the years Miss Marple must have appeared many times as an important witness for the prosecution, yet these expeditions are never mentioned. "Naturally, nothing was said of Miss Marple's share in the business. She herself would have been horrified at the thought of such a thing," wrote Leonard Clement in *The Murder at the Vicarage*. One wonders, nevertheless, whether Scotland Yard would have permitted this ace up its sleeve to go unplayed for more than one or two cases. And what an interesting witness she would have been, a sweet-faced old lady, dressed in black or speckled tweed, sitting very upright in the witness box and beginning her testimony with flutterings and apologies and something like this: "Please forgive me. So apt, I know, to fly off at a tangent. But one thing does remind one of another."

Eleven

"My Nephew, the Author," and Other Relatives and Friends

The one with white fluffy hair and the knitting?
. . . Everybody's universal great-aunt.
—Chief Inspector Davy,
At Bertram's Hotel

It's lucky that Miss Marple's cousin's sister's aunt's brother-in-law or whatever it was lives near here," remarked Giles Reed in *Sleeping Murder* of the pleasant old lady who had providentially turned up to help him and his wife solve a murder. In fact, his impression of Miss Marple belonging to an extended family was quite wrong. Though her childhood, as we have seen, was blessed with a healthy share of interesting aunts and benign uncles, in later years she seems to have had very few living relatives or, at least, ones that are ever mentioned. It is only her dear nephew Raymond, his wife Joan, and their two sons who figure in the detective years, and very important they were. Perhaps they were enough.

Raymond was presumably the son of Miss Marple's sister, who is mentioned only once: "My sister and I had a German governess." That there is no further reference to this sister, and given Raymond's steady affection and financial support of his Aunt Jane over the years, it could be speculated that this sister died as a young widow and that Miss Marple brought Raymond up. And did she bring up a niece as well, the tiresome Mabel Denman, rescued from suspicion of murdering her husband in "The Thumbmark of St. Peter"? And was this Mabel, who never appears again in Marpelian literature, Raymond's sister? We are never told. There were other nieces as well, referred to once or twice in passing—"Now I like to keep all the pictures of my nephews and nieces as babies" . . . "a young niece of mine not long before had hurried her child off to a very well-known specialist in skin diseases"—but they are never mentioned by name; Raymond reigned supreme.

In Miss Marple's life as a detective, Raymond West first appeared in the Tuesday Night Club short stories. Wrote Agatha Christie in her autobiography:

I gave Miss Marple five colleagues for the series of six stories. First was her nephew; a modern novelist who dealt in strong meat in his books, incest, sex, and sordid descriptions of bedrooms and lavatory equipment—the stark side of life was what Raymond West saw. His dear, pretty, old, fluffy Aunt Jane he treated with an indulgent kindness as one who knew nothing of the world.

This game of indulgence, one for the other, was something Raymond and Miss Marple loved to play:

"My dear Aunt Jane, why must you bury your head in the sand like a very delightful ostrich? All bound up in this idyllic rural life of yours. REAL LIFE—that's what matters."

"He writes very clever books, I believe, though people are not really nearly so unpleasant as he makes out. Clever young men know so little of life, don't you think?"

Despite Miss Marple's reservations, it is clear that Raymond was a successful novelist and earned a comfortable living by his pen. In the early stories and in *The Murder at the Vicarage* he was a promising *enfant terrible,* "a rather exquisite young man," coming down from London to spend the occasional weekend.

"My nephew," she explained, "My nephew, Raymond West, the author. He is coming down today. Such a to-do. I have to see to everything myself. You cannot trust a maid to air a bed properly, and we must, of course, have a meat meal tonight."

Nothing was too good for Raymond. In return, as his life expanded to include a wife and children, a house in Chelsea, and a home in the country, and his morning mail to contain at least six requests for his well-known autograph, he did not forget his Aunt Jane.

In the Tuesday Night Club cycle Raymond became engaged to Joyce Lamprière, the artist, but he eventually married another artist, Joan.* Joan West's art—she "paints those very remarkable pictures of square people with curious bulges"—was as inexplicable to Miss Marple as Raymond's fiction, but she became very fond of her. A picture of this fashionable young couple is provided in *Sleeping Murder* when Gwenda Reed, their cousin by marriage from New Zealand, visits them in London:

> It was not their fault that Gwenda found them secretly rather alarming. Raymond, with his odd appearance, rather like a pouncing raven, his sweep of hair and his sudden crescendos of quite incomprehensible conversation, left Gwenda round-eyed and nervous. Both he and Joan seemed to talk a language of their own.

As time went by the Wests produced two sons, Lionel and David, and mellowed. In the mid-1950s Raymond is described as "softening a little with the advent of middle age," and in the mid-1960s "Miss Marple reflected with a qualm that Joan must now be close on fifty." Their sons grew up. One of them—it is not made clear which—became very interested in racing cars, and David, in British Railways, was of help to Miss Marple in her search for a body in *What Mrs. McGillicuddy Saw!*

---

* It is possible that Joyce and Joan were the same person, with the difference in name arising from a change of mind or a slight error on Agatha Christie's part.

From our point of view the important thing about the Wests is that they were very good to Miss Marple. "Raymond was very fond of his old aunt and was constantly devising treats for her." His generosity relieved her of the worries of a small income and freed her to devote her attention to that most interesting pursuit, the solving of murders. When she was ill and very old, he provided nurses and housekeepers. When he thought she needed a change, he arranged holidays.

In time he even came to respect her ability as a detective and to acknowledge that she might have some passing acquaintance with the twentieth century. When assuring her that a friend would take good care of her house while she was away in the West Indies, he described him to Miss Marple as house proud, a queer. "He had paused, slightly embarrassed—but surely even dear old Aunt Jane must have heard of queers."

Raymond trained Miss Marple well. Over the years a number of people saw in her the epitome of what they thought an aunt should be and claimed her accordingly. There was "the handsome and well-gaitered Bishop of Westchester," for example, "with memories of himself as a child in a Hampshire vicarage calling out lustily 'Be a crocodile now, Aunty Janie. Be a crocodile and eat me.' " To the crusty Colonel Melchett, coping with a difficult case, her "you'll have no trouble, I can assure you" was "the tone in which his favorite aunt had once assured him that he could not fail to pass his entrance examination into Sandhurst." She had a similar effect on police officers. In *A Pocket Full of Rye* she nodded at

Inspector Neele "encouragingly, as an aunt might have encouraged a bright nephew who was going in for a scholarship exam," and she reminded Detective-Inspector Craddock, who came to call her Aunt Jane in a number of his cases, of "his own great aunt Emma. She had finally told him that his nose twitched when he was about to tell a lie." Joyce Lemprière of the Tuesday Night Club called Miss Marple aunt, as did the middle-aged Mildred Strete of *Murder with Mirrors*—a faint shock to Miss Marple. But she did not find it shocking to shamelessly invent a fictitious nephew, Denzil, to try to get her hands on a promising piece of evidence in *A Caribbean Mystery*.

One is given the impression that Miss Marple was a godmother to a number of people, but we are only told specifically of two: the Rhodes baby in "Miss Marple Tells a Story" whose father she saved from a charge of murder, and her favorite godchild, Bunch Harmon. Bunch's father had once been the vicar of St. Mary Mead and both her parents were old friends of Miss Marple's. Optimistically christened Diana, "the roundness of [her] form and face had early led to the soubriquet of 'Bunch.' " She dressed terribly—"Her battered felt hat was stuck on the back of her head in a vague attempt to be fashionable and she had put on a rather limp frilly blouse instead of her usual pullover." Everyone loved her for her good humor and enthusiasm. Miss Marple saw something else in her, however: "You have a lot of common sense, Bunch, and you're very intelligent." Bunch was married to the Reverend Julian Harmon, vicar of Chipping Cleghorn, and she happily presided over a huge, drafty rectory devoid of central heating and labor-saving devices. Her husband, an endearing, scholarly man, often confused his parishioners with his esoteric sermons and read Gibbon to his young wife in the evenings.

The life of this goddaughter and her husband in Chipping Cleghorn must often have reminded Miss Marple of the one led in the vicarage next door to her in St. Mary Mead, a vicarage probably familiar to Bunch from her own childhood. Griselda Clement was better dressed and more sophisticated than Bunch, but she was equally happy with her middle-aged, absentminded clergyman and just as casual a housekeeper. Wrote the Reverend Leonard Clement of his wife:

> Griselda is nearly twenty years younger than myself. She is most distractingly pretty and quite incapable of taking anything seriously. She is incompetent in every way and extremely trying to live with. She treats the parish as a kind of huge joke arranged for her amusement. I have endeavored to form her mind and failed.

Rev. Leonard Clement was not such a prig as all this might suggest. He possessed a low-key humor of his own and a great sense of the ridiculous. Unworldly and slightly pompous he may have appeared to many of his parishioners, but, shut away in his study after one of the vicarage's awful meals (" 'Greens,' said the sloppy maid, and thrust a cracked dish at him in a truculent manner"), he wrote a great many amusing and perceptive things about St. Mary Mead and its inhabitants.

"I have a steadying influence coming into my life," Griselda announced to her husband as the giddy events of *The Murder at the Vicarage* were drawing to a close. The steadying influence, young Leonard, makes his first appearance in *The Body in the Library* while crawling across the hearthrug with a mother who

> butted her son three times in the stomach, so that he caught hold of her hair and pulled it with gleeful yells. They then rolled over and over in a grand rough and tumble until the door opened and the vicarage maid announced to the most influential parishioner, who didn't like children, "Missus is in here."

Young Leonard is mentioned as a sticky little boy in "The Case of the Perfect Maid" and reappears again, some twenty years later, in *What Mrs. McGillicuddy Saw!*, where his passion for maps makes him a useful consultant for Miss Marple. At this time, the late 1950s, the Clements were still living next door to Miss Marple, Griselda looking "strangely young and blooming to be inhabiting the shabby old vicarage." That year, as usual, Miss Marple was a guest at their Christmas dinner (had the cooking improved over the years? one wonders), but five years later, in *The Mirror Crack'd*, the Clements had moved away. Griselda kept in touch, though, and "that attractive baby of hers was a strapping young man now, and with a very good job." Perhaps Leonard Clement had by this time died. Whatever the reason for his departure from St. Mary Mead, it is a great pity he was not on hand to chronicle the goings on and murders at Gossington Hall during its occupancy by the film star Marina Gregg.

A quite different vicarage wife than Bunch and Griselda was Miss Marple's terrifying friend Mrs. Dane Calthrop of Lymstock. She only appears in one book, but she is unforgettable. Married to the remote and scholarly Reverend Caleb Dane Calthrop, "she was a woman of character and of almost Olympian knowledge." Of her, Jerry Burton, the narrator of *The Moving Finger*, wrote:

> I have never seen a woman more indifferent to her material surroundings. On hot days she would stride about clad in Harris tweed, and in rain or even sleet, I have seen her absent-mindedly race down the village street in a cotton dress of printed poppies. She had a long thin well-bred face like a greyhound, and a most devastating sincerity of speech.

Mrs. Dane Calthrop was always saying the most riveting things: "Caleb has absolutely no taste for fornication. He never has had. So lucky, being a clergyman"; or, exhibiting a lobster, "Have you ever seen anything so unlike Mr. Pye? . . . very virile and handsome, isn't it?" This was perhaps why Miss Marple, her guest in *The Moving Finger*, appeared uncharacteristically subdued. Probably *everyone* became uncharacteristically subdued in Mrs. Dane Calthrop's presence.

In contrast to the awesome Dane Calthrops, more comfortable friends than Dolly and Arthur Bantry would be difficult to imagine. The owners for many years of Gossington Hall, they were first persuaded to invite Miss Marple to a dinner party by Sir Henry Clithering. After a cycle of murder-guessing dinner parties, Dolly and Miss Marple became the greatest of friends. It was to Miss Marple that Dolly immediately turned when the body of a very young woman was discovered one morning in her husband's library.

Colonel Arthur Bantry, the victim of this horrible joke, was a kindly, bluff man who loved farming, the Conservative Party, and the country life he led as master of Gossington Hall. "Looking at pigs and things always soothes him if he's been upset." Any interruptions were fiercely resented. He hated music, for example ("Tone deaf, poor dear. His face, when some kind friend took us to the opera!"), trendy people invading St. Mary Mead ("shrieking, noisy crowds"), and going to Ascot.

Dolly Bantry was Miss Marple's ally and confidant for at least thirty years and was as much fun after all that time, still going strong as a plump and amiable widow, as she had been at the beginning. "Vodka ought really to be thrown straight down the throat," she advised a timid drinker in *The Mirror Crack'd*. Her real obsession, however, was flowers. In her day she had kept "the best iris garden of any in the county," and on the very first page of *The Body in the Library* we find her dreaming:

> Her sweet peas had just taken a First at the flower show. The vicar, dressed in cassock and surplice, was giving out the prizes in church. His wife wandered past, dressed in a bathing suit . . .

Strategically placed on the High Street opposite the shops and the church were three pretty houses, "Queen Anne and Georgian." They belonged to Miss Jane Marple, Miss Amanda Hartnell, and Miss Caroline Wetherby. It was a firmly held conviction in St. Mary Mead that nothing of interest or scandal ever occurred that was not instantly known and discussed in one or the other of their prim drawing rooms. St. Mary Mead was right; these three were indeed a formidable alliance, for they shared characteristics of insatiable curiosity and an unrelenting belief in the depravity of human nature. Over the course of her long career, in turning her talents to sterner stuff, Miss Marple rather outgrew Miss Wetherby and Miss Hartnell but afternoon tea, with the three of them gathered together, remained an important event. Whatever else was happening in her life, Miss Marple liked to keep in touch with what was going on in St. Mary Mead, criminal or not. No one knew better than Miss Wetherby and Miss Hartnell.

Of the two, Miss Wetherby was the quieter and plainer. In *The Body in the Library* she is uncharitably described as "a long-nosed, acidulated spinster," and in *The Murder at the Vicarage* the Vicar writes of her closing "her thin lips disapprovingly." He thought her more soft-hearted than Miss Hartnell, however, who appeared jolly on the surface ("What ho, within there!" she was wont to cry in a bass voice) but was a dragon underneath, particularly with the poor, whom she visited indefatigably. "And four of my poorer parishioners declared open rebellion against Miss Hartnell," reported the Vicar. In one of the later books, *The Mirror Crack'd*, Miss Wetherby had passed away but Miss Hartnell was still hard at it, "fighting progress to the last gasp."

Is it possible that Miss Marple had the three of them in mind when she envisaged *Macbeth*'s three witches at their most dangerous as three perfectly ordinary old women, the kind of old lady who flutters around "the dear Vicar, and embroiders awful slippers for him, and gives him bedsocks for Christmas"?

Miss Hartnell's house stood on one side of Miss Marple's; on the other was Dr. Haydock's. From it he fared forth to minister to the ills of the village and examine those of its citizens whose lives had been prematurely shortened, for Dr. Haydock, besides being the village physician, was also its police surgeon. Over the years he appeared in many Miss Marple books and short stories, in the early ones as "a big, fine, strapping fellow, with an honest, rugged face," and in later ones as elderly and semi-retired, yet another indication of how enormously long was Miss Marple's own old age. Each of them greatly admired the other, though sometimes their convictions diverged—Dr. Haydock was no churchgoer, for example, and was against capital punishment—but they were both firm believers in good common sense, which was probably why Miss Marple would have no other doctor. For Miss Emily Skinner, for instance, languishing in bed in her flat in Old Hall, he prescribed a mixture of asafoetida and valerian, "the stock remedy for malingerers in the army!" For Miss Marple's occasional malingering he had more sympathy. As a fellow professional he realized that she often had her own reason. "Let's hear why you sent for me," he once told her. "Just tell me what it's to be and I'll repeat it after you." He was her firm friend and ally from first to last and always encouraged her, even in her extreme old age, to keep on sleuthing.

A number of other people deserve mention as friends of Miss Marple's. Her very oldest ones, in years of friendship, were undoubtedly two Americans, Ruth Van Rydock and her sister, Carrie Louise Serrocold. As we have seen, the three of them had met while schoolgirls together in Florence, "herself, the pink and white English girl from a Cathedral Close." Carrie Louise eventually came to live in England, but it was the cosmopolitan Ruth, on her periodic swoops upon London, whom Miss Marple saw more often:

> It was practically impossible when looking at Mrs. Van Rydock to imagine what she would be like in a natural state. Everything that money could do had been done for her—reinforced by diet, massage, and constant exercises.
>
> Ruth Van Rydock looked humourously at her friend.
>
> "Do you think most people would guess, Jane, that you and I are practically the same age?"
>
> Miss Marple responded loyally.
>
> "Not for a moment, I'm sure," she said reassuringly. "I'm afraid, you know, that I look every minute of my age!"

Two other old friends were Mrs. Price Ridley, who was a terrible pain in the neck, and Mrs. McGillicuddy, who was very nice. Mrs. Price Ridley, widowed, rich, and interfering, lived next to the vicarage. Righteous indignation was her specialty and surged constantly into expression from the depths of her ample bosom; at times only the swift intervention of a glass of damson gin prevented her complete collapse. In her formidable hats she made frequent appearances at tea and scandal. Elspeth McGillicuddy, "short and stout," was a more welcome sight. She did not live in St. Mary Mead but visited her old friend Jane from time to time. Miss Marple was very fond of her son Roderick and had once helped him over a matter of money missing from a school locker. In *What Mrs. McGillicuddy Saw!*, Elspeth cuts short a visit to Ceylon to come home and help Jane unmask a murderer.

Besides "Dear Raymond," the most important men in Miss Marple's life were, not surprisingly, officers of the law. And very fond of her they were. They usually started off dismissing her as a dithery old lady and ended up as fans. Three stand out: Colonel Melchett, Sir Henry Clithering, and Detective-Inspector Craddock.

Colonel Melchett, "an irascible-looking man with a habit of tugging at his short red moustache," was the chief constable of the county. In this position he supervised the investigations of a number of murders, all in due course solved by Miss Marple. Inspector Slack, his assistant, minded this very much, but the gruff colonel took it all in his stride. "She's a very sharp old lady," he said of Miss Marple.

Sir Henry Clithering, debonair and "one of the best brains in England," shared this opinion: "just the finest detective God ever made—natural genius cultivated in a suitable soil." People were forever turning up in Miss Marple's life to tell her what a wonderful detective Sir Henry Clithering thought she was, and the mere mention of his name reduced her to blushings and flutterings. "Dear Sir Henry . . . Always so kind. Really I'm not at all clever—just, perhaps, a *slight* knowledge of human nature—living, you know, in a *village*." They began their friendship at the very beginning of Miss Marple's career in the Tuesday Night Club days, worked together to solve a number of murders, and were still speaking admiringly of each other in *Nemesis*, Miss Marple's last recorded case.

Dermot Craddock was Sir Henry's godson, passed on to her with many recommendations. Miss Marple adored him: "Her candid blue eyes swept over the manly proportions and handsome face of Detective-Inspector Craddock with truly feminine Victorian appreciation." He became "my dear boy" and she became his "Aunty." All this gushing notwithstanding, the two made a formidable team, as any number of murderers were to discover. Patient, open-minded, and reassuring, Detective-Inspector Craddock was an ideal collaborator. He was also very astute. "Consult Miss M. for latest gossip," he wrote in a list outlining the steps of a criminal investigation.

Without doubt Miss Marple's most extraordinary friend was old Jason Rafiel. He turned up in her third-to-last case, *A Caribbean Mystery*, and was dead and buried before her last one, *Nemesis*, began, but he made a huge impact. That was his style. A "strong man, an obstinate man—a very rich man," he had made millions out of a chain of supermarkets in the north of England. When Miss Marple met him during his holiday in the West Indies he was a disconcerting sight, "incredibly desiccated, his bones draped with festoons of dry skin." He was also incredibly rude, with no sympathy at all for "knitting wool and tittle-tattle." Altogether an unlikely friend for Miss Marple, one would have thought, but when she unhesitatingly broke into his room in the middle of the night to enlist him as her ally in a case of murder, she won his lasting respect: "To Miss Jane Marple, resident in the village of St. Mary Mead . . . I want you to investigate a certain crime," read his last will and testament a number of years later. With this, a generous expense account, and a commission of twenty thousand pounds, Miss Marple triumphantly ended her career.

Twelve

Little Maids All In a Row

And sure enough poor Florrie was in trouble—
the gentlemanly assistant at the hairdresser's.
Fortunately it was in good time, and I was
able to have a little talk with him, and they
had a very nice wedding and settled down quite
happily.

—Miss Marple, *A Murder is Announced*

Miss Marple lacked the luxury enjoyed by Hercule
Poirot, with his manservant George; Lord Peter
Wimsey, with his Bunter; and Albert Campion,
with his Magersfontein Lugg. Instead she had house-
maids, one after another after another:

Rather simple, some of them had been, and frequently
adenoidal, and Amy distinctly moronic. They had gos-

siped and chattered with the other maids in the village and walked out with the fishmonger's assistant, or the undergardener at the Hall, or one of Mr. Barnes the grocer's numerous assistants. Miss Marple's mind went back over them affectionately thinking of all the little woolly coats she had knitted for their subsequent offspring.

"My little maid Janet," Gwen, "my little maid with red hair," "Edna, Miss Marple's little maid," little Amy, Annie, Clara, Kitty, Gladys, Alice, Ethel, Emily, Evelyn, Edith—they came and went, little maids all in a row. "I usually have very young maids," said Miss Marple. They came to her from St. Faith's Orphanage, "a very well run place" (Miss Marple sat on its committee), "though sadly short of funds. We do our best for the girls there, try to give them a good training and all that."

Fresh from the orphanage, what sort of training did they receive in the neat little house on the High Street of St. Mary Mead? Very thorough, you may be sure. "Ernie always says to me, 'Everything what's good you learned from that Miss Marple of yours that you were in service with,' " an ex-maid once told Miss Marple. They wore uniforms, of course, and neat white aprons. They learned to wait at table and polish the silver, air the sheets properly and turn the mattresses, wash up without breaking the china, and dust without breaking the ornaments. They learned to address her as Miss or Ma'am and to answer the door with "Not at home" when she did not wish to be disturbed. They learned simple unadventuresome cookery: herrings, kippers, boiled eggs, scones, "meat meals" for gentlemen, damson jam, and damson gin. One imagines a constant apprenticeship going on at Miss Marple's and a steady procession of competent little maids emerging from her tutelage to be quickly snatched up as parlormaids by richer mistresses, or as wives by lucky grocery assistants.

Sometimes, alas, things went awry. Kitty claimed to have done the spring cleaning but there were spider webs on the cornice. Emily couldn't be trusted to air a bed properly. And worse—little Janet told fibs. "She'd explain quite convincingly that the mice had eaten the end of a cake and give herself away by smirking as she left the room." Alice embezzled the accounts. Ethel, "a very good-looking girl and obliging in every way," went on to Lady Ashton and stole two diamond brooches and cut the lace off her underwear! Ghoulish tales of such entrepreneurial maids, traitors to the code, were told in hushed voices over afternoon tea. Indeed, "servants were the main topic of conversation in St. Mary Mead," at least among the middle classes, and there is a wonderful Miss Marple short story, "The Case of the Perfect Maid," in which appears a paragon, Mary Higgins, who embodies every virtue the most discriminating mistress could ever hope to find: forty years of age, excellent references, asked only the most modest of wages, loved the country, dressed neatly, spoke in a "proper, inaudible, respectful voice," cooked, waited on table, cleaned to perfection, was splendid with invalids, and so on. As this marvel belonged to the unpopular Misses Skinner, "great was the chagrin of the village." Fortunately, for the peace of mind of all, she turned out to be a fiction.

Some little maids one loved despite their faults. Here is Miss Marple telling Bunch Harmon about a hopeless one:

> "She was no good at all at waiting at table. Put everything on the table crooked, mixed up the kitchen knives with the dining-room ones, and her cap (this was a long time ago, dear) her cap was *never* straight."
>
> Bunch adjusted her hat automatically.
>
> "Anything else?" she demanded anxiously.
>
> "I kept her because she was so pleasant to have about the house—and because she used to make me laugh."

This maid turned out well in the end, marrying a Baptist minister. Not so Gladys Martin, "quite a decent sort of girl but very nearly half-witted. The adenoidal type." Gladys strayed too far from St. Mary Mead and her heartbreak over Fred, the fishmonger's boy. "Oh, madam, I don't like to ask it of you but if you could only come here and help me they'd listen to you and you were always so kind to me" was her cry for help in a letter that arrived on Miss Marple's hall table too late to prevent Gladys's murder in *A Pocket Full of Rye*. But let a murderer beware who does away so lightly with one of Miss Marple's little graduates, however adenoidal—an elderly lady with a bird's wing on her hat will appear from nowhere to avenge her.

Two wonderful ex-maids, yet another Gladys and Faithful Florence, "that grenadier of a parlourmaid," were pressed into service long after they had left St. Mary Mead. In "Sanctuary" the successful Gladys, married and living in London, helped Miss Marple foil a pair of jewel thieves; and in *What Mrs. McGillicuddy Saw!* Faithful Florence, living in Brackhampton and taking in respectable boarders, provided her with a hideout amidst "china dogs and presents from Margate."

The little maids—alas, how one mourned them in later years, even the cheeky, sloppy ones. Their rapid disappearance as a species is inexorably recorded in Marpelian literature, heralded by a little bat squeak from Miss Wetherby in the 1930s—"one doesn't let a servant go nowadays unless it's something rather grave"—and ending with "frenzied appeals for Domestic Help" in the personal columns by 1950. Then followed sad days for most of Miss Marple's contemporaries:

> . . . they had that worried harried look of domestic anxieties with which they are too tired to cope, or they rushed around to committees and tried to appear bustling and competent, or they dyed their hair gentian blue, or wore wigs, and their hands were not the hands she remembered, tapering, delicate hands—they were harsh from washing up and detergents.

Painful attempts were made to fill the vacuum. Of course one could no longer hope for muslin caps and aprons, or the finer points of bed making, but one was still ill-prepared for the humility required to retain one's new treasure, the daily. In *A Murder Is Announced* Mrs. Sweetenham tried to persuade her son to stop taking the Marxist *Daily Worker* lest Mrs. Finch, "a grim-looking female in an aged velvet beret," take umbrage and not come to clean at all. Or one might try to get foreign domestic help, best exemplified by Miss Blacklock's Mitzi, a far cry indeed from the neat little maids of yesteryear, in *A Murder Is Announced*:

> Through the door there surged a tempestuous young woman with a well-developed bosom heaving under a tight jersey. She had on a dirndl skirt of a bright colour and had greasy dark plaits wound round and round her head. Her eyes were dark and flashing.

Or, if one was rich or desperate enough, one might try to hire someone like Lucy Eyelesbarrow, an extremely able and well-educated young woman, who knew that "to gain money one must exploit shortage." To this end she had deserted the prospects of a brilliant academic career to become a professional housekeeper. Since she enjoyed frequent changes of scene (she had a sense of humor as well as everything else), her rule was to limit each engagement to a month or less.

> Lucy Eyelesbarrow did everthing, saw to everything, arranged everything. She was unbelievably competent in every conceivable sphere. She looked after elderly parents, accepted the care of young children, nursed the sickly, cooked divinely, got on well with any old crusted servants there might happen to be (there usually weren't), was tactful with impossible people, soothed habitual drunkards, was wonderful with dogs.

Miss Marple hired her once to work in someone else's home. "You were engaged by an elderly lady to obtain a post here and to search the house and grounds for *a dead body?"* demanded an incredulous Inspector Bacon in *What Mrs. McGillicuddy Saw!* She had been and she did. It was all in a day's work for Lucy.

To have a Lucy Eyelesbarrow could happen only once or twice in a lifetime, and then it was back to the chars, the *au pairs*, or the dailies. It says much for Miss Marple's adaptability in old age that, unlike many of her contemporaries, she weathered the transition from the resident little maid to the casual helper with considerable élan, which brings us to the subject of her final and greatest triumph in the domestic arena, Cherry Baker.

It was a victory snatched from the jaws of defeat, for Cherry entered Miss Marple's life in *The Mirror Crack'd* at a most difficult time. Her garden, because of her rheumatism, was at the mercy of Old Laycock, a jobbing gardener who drank endless cups of tea instead of deep trenching the sweet peas properly, and her everyday life, because of an attack of bronchitis, was at the mercy of Miss Knight, a live-in housekeeper and companion (provided by dear Raymond, of course) whose very voice was enough to set Miss Marple's teeth on edge:

> "Here we are!" she exclaimed with a kind of beaming boisterousness, meant to cheer and enliven the sad twilight of the aged. "I hope we've had our little snooze?"

The indignities of old age! To be treated like a slightly retarded child! Oh, for the little maids of yesteryear with their respectful "Ma'ams."

Enter Cherry Baker, a daily—at first sight as unlikely a successor to the little Amys and Claras of the past as could possibly be imagined, with her rakish plastic aprons and her belief that all housecleaning could be accomplished with a vacuum cleaner ("What, get down on my knees with a dustpan and brush?"). She lived in the Development, that ominous new encroachment on the old St. Mary Mead, and she represented yet another new wave of domestics, young married women: "Owing to the insidious snares of Hire Purchase, they were always in need of ready money, though their husbands all earned good wages; and so they came and did housework and cooking."

It was a new kind of housework, and Miss Marple was clever enough to turn a blind eye to mattresses unturned, hastily made beds, and the disconcerting sight of her old Worcester subjected to detergent (she quietly purchased a modern tea service with no gilt on it). In return for this benignity, she acquired in Cherry someone who was quick and intelligent, took telephone messages correctly, caught on at once to the tradesmen's books, reported the news of the village, sang at her work with a tuneful voice, privately referred to Miss Knight as "old jelly-bag," and was generally great fun to have around.

Together they pulled off a great coup—they got rid of Miss Knight, who threatened to linger on indefinitely (though Miss Marple's bronchitis had cleared up quite nicely while solving the murders at Gossington Hall) following Dr. Haydock's annoying pronouncement that Miss Marple must no longer stay alone at night. "It's no good your bullying me. . . . You're an old lady and you've got to be looked after in a proper manner." The grim prospect of a future of nurse companions was averted by Cherry's unexpected proposal that she and her husband sell their boring and expensive semidetached in the Development to come and live permanently with Miss Marple in the old servants' rooms over the kitchen:

> "Jim could fix things for you any time—you know, plumbing or a bit of carpentry. And I'd look after you every bit as well as your Miss Knight does. I know you think I'm a bit slap-dash—but I'd try and take trouble with the beds and the washing-up—and I'm getting quite a dab at cooking. Did Beef Stroganoff last night, it's quite easy, really."

So the bargain was struck and a very good one it was, for nine years later, in *Nemesis*, Cherry and her husband are still in residence.

> "You take very good care of me, Cherry," said Miss Marple.
> "Got to," said Cherry, in her usual idiom. "Good people are scarce."

Thus, in very old age, while still knitting little pullovers for the children—and probably the grandchildren—of the little maids all in a row, Miss Marple cleverly achieved, like Lord Peter Wimsey, Albert Campion, and Hercule Poirot, the servant who suited her perfectly.

Thirteen

Miss Marple as Sleuth

"You have a theory?" asked Inspector Neele, "as to who put the taxine into Mr. Fortescue's marmalade."

"It isn't a theory," said Miss Marple. "I know."
—*A Pocket Full of Rye*

In Miss Marple's last case, *Nemesis*, a solemn lawyer in charge of a will commissioning her to solve an unnamed crime cannot resist asking, "have you had— oh, how shall I put it?—any connection with crime or the investigation of crime?" It was rather like asking Jacques Cousteau if he was familiar with life under the sea or Yehudi Menuhin if he understood the violin. She had, after all, solved dozens of murders, not to mention any number of burglaries, blackmails, embezzlements, and other assorted nastiness. Still, faced with a very elderly lady up from the country and dressed in a tweed suit and a velvet toque, Mr. Broadribb's question could be forgiven. How could she possibly know anything about the investigation of crime?

It was quite simple, she said, over and over again. She had a fine sense of evil, and when it was abroad she never accepted anything important or interesting anyone told her without corroborating evidence.

> "The trouble in this case is that everybody has been much too credulous and believing. You simply cannot afford to believe everything that people tell you. When there's anything fishy about, I never believe anyone at all."

For her knowledge of human nature she drew on that valuable microcosm, St. Mary Mead.

But this attitude would never have raised her from the level of an ordinary village gossip, who always believed the worst, to the superb detective she became had it not been for two other factors: her great intelligence and the inspired crimes Agatha Christie gave her to solve.

People, especially criminals and policemen, frequently underestimated her intelligence. When she surprised them they were apt to conclude, because she was a fluffy old village lady, that her successes were due to feminine intuition—a sort of lucky quantum leap, based on guesses and premonitions, to the right answer. In this they were all quite wrong. Miss Marple had an excellent mind. Logical and inquiring, she would have made, if born to another time or sphere, a first-rate scientist. First she collected the facts and then she made her hypothesis.

"If you have a theory that fits every fact—well, then it must be the right one," she said. The great fun of Miss Marple is that she tended to make it all look so muddling as she went along—a shrewd weapon in her arsenal.

She loved solving murders. It was a vocation with her. Raymond remarked, "Some commit murder, some get mixed up in murder, others have murder thrust upon them. My Aunt Jane comes into the third category." He was only partially right, however. Though murders did often spontaneously occur in a place and time where Miss Marple happened to be, equally as often she sought them out as soon as she caught the slightest whiff of them through her grapevine of relatives and friends, often traveling considerable distances—sometimes feigning illnesses or coincidences—to arrive, invited or not, on the scene. She enjoyed solving problems and she liked catching criminals. "I am," she once said, "in my own way an emissary of justice."

To justice she brought some very ruthless and cunning murderers indeed—middle-class murderers, usually, who killed violently and ingeniously, often more than once and usually from motives of greed. They shot, strangled, stabbed or poisoned their victims and hid or left the bodies in the most unexpected places—in a vicar's study, for example, or stuffed into a Greek sarcophagus, or buried in a prim garden. Had it not been for Miss Marple, they would have got away with their crimes, and, in many cases, innocent people would have been tried in their stead. How did she do it? What were her methods?

To begin with, she wore a good disguise. How shamelessly unthreatening she was! No notebook, no car, no assistants, no official capacity—all she appeared to be was a sweet old lady, sometimes even a *dotty* old lady, "talking in a childish and garrulous manner." It was a wonderful cover. Witness her, in *A Pocket Full of Rye,* gaining access to the scene of a murder, the Fortescue home, which has been sealed off to the public:

> Though an army of reporters and photographers were being kept at bay by the police, Miss Marple was allowed to drive in without question, so impossible would it have been to believe that she was anyone but an elderly relative of the family.

Her credentials as a harmless old lady established, she could then turn her energies to conversation and observation: "Three plain, two purl, slip one, knit two together . . . And your second husband, my dear?"

She listened:

> There must be no show of special interest in her eyes when she heard about a death. Not at all. Almost automatically she was sure she could come up with the right response such as, "Oh dear me, how *very* sad!" She would have to find out relationships, incidents, life stories, see if any suggestive incidents would pop up, so to speak . . . Something they could know about, talk about, or were pretty sure to talk about. Anyway, there would be *something* here, some clue, some pointer.

And she watched:

> Although her face registered nothing, the keen eyes behind her glasses had watched three people in a simultaneous manner as she had trained herself to do for many

years now, when wishing to observe her neighbours either in church, mothers' meetings, or at other public functions in St. Mary Mead when she had been on the track of some interesting piece of news or gossip.

Like any good detective, she also did her legwork. Dinner-party mysteries and everyday sleuthings in St. Mary Mead ("the absent-minded postman—the gardener who worked on Whit Monday—and that very curious affair of the summer weight combinations") kept her in training. When the real thing came along, she worked hard. A typical day on a case saw her, in *A Murder Is Announced*, dropping in for coffee at the Bluebird Café, having tea with Miss Blacklock, sherry with Miss Hinchliffe and Miss Murgatroyd, and stopping by to admire Mrs. Swettenham's garden and Colonel Easterbrook's curios. Canvassing and collecting for good causes was another good cover. "Sale of Work?" queried a suspect platinum blonde when Miss Marple appeared at her door with a little black book.

Just happening to appear at someone's door, or bumping into someone by chance, took careful planning. To casually encounter Gwenda Reed on the esplanade at Dillmouth, in *Sleeping Murder*, required being declared ill enough by Dr. Haydock to need a few weeks of sea air. To collide with Esther Walters just outside the supermarket in Alton, in *Nemesis*, entailed hiring one of Inch's taxis and drivers for half a day and telling a lot of fibs.

Which brings us to duplicity. Once again, who could believe an old lady capable of *so much*? Of sending Miss

Knight off on a false errand? Of "abstracting" Miss Politt's tape measure? Of persuading her old friend Elspeth McGillicuddy to ask to go to the bathroom when she didn't need to (" 'It's very cold weather,' Miss Marple pointed out, 'and after all, you might have eaten something that disagreed with you' "). Of she herself, Jane Marple, pretending to choke on a fish bone? Duplicity was a specialty of Miss Marple's.

She also, like any other detective, did her homework. That is, she *thought*. Sometimes she went for a walk: "I just put one foot in front of the other and wonder about things." Sometimes she was discovered talking to herself. Sometimes she even dropped stitches. Sometimes she made abrupt little lists: "Lamp. Violets. Where is bottle of aspirin?" Sometimes she got up in the middle of the night to make notes. "I must try to make as logical a survey as I can of this project which I have undertaken," she wrote in *Nemesis*.

Logic. This was how Miss Marple solved her murders, although the word is not the first that one would associate with her twittering old-maid image. There is no talk of the little gray cells in these books, but, when the endings are unraveled and the killers brought to justice, it is clear that she had first collected all the available facts by all the available means, viewed them in light of her vast knowledge of erring human nature in the anthill of St. Mary Mead, and then applied logic to reach a conclusion. Using this method she was able to disentangle the most complicated misdirections her villains could devise: false identities, impersonations, double bluffs, misleading coincidences, suppressed wills, obscure motives, conjuring tricks, irreconcilable facts, unassailable alibis, and so forth. Inspector Craddock once suggested she did it all by guess-work:

"*Not* guesswork," said Miss Marple . . . "It's all in Mark Twain. The boy who found the horse. He just imagined where he would go if he were a horse and he went there and there was the horse."

Once she had deduced who the murderer was, she often set a trap to clinch the evidence. Here she was at her very best, an inspired stage manager, "looking more alert than ever, much as a fox terrier might look waiting at a rat-hole."

These traps were always very exciting, sometimes violent, and usually ended with hysterical confessions from astonished murderers who had no inkling, until the last moment, that Miss Marple had had them under a microscope all along. "She's a very harmless old creature," said one very dangerous and Least Likely Person shortly before being unmasked as a killer by an elaborate scenario. "You devilish old hag," cried another, tricked into recreating the scene of the crime. "My little plan," Miss Marple was apt to call such occasions.

These little plans were usually carried out with the bemused connivance of the police. Obviously *someone* had to be on the scene at the end to arrest the criminal. Law-abiding, in no way did Miss Marple regard herself as a vigilante. She generally worked along with the pre-siding officer throughout the case—whether he liked it or not—and these relationships tended to follow a pattern: initial condescension toward a funny old lady who for some reason kept popping up in the course of the investigation, an interim stage of dawning suspicion that she might be a great deal brighter and more dangerous than she first appeared, and a final capitulation and acknowledgement of a finer mind. It was a bitter pill, but the swallowing was always helped along by auntlike coos of encouragement from Miss Marple, who liked to keep these police officers on her side, for who knew when she might need them again? "The great thing to avoid is having in any way a trustful mind," she once lectured an experienced inspector from Scotland Yard. "Miss Marple is capable of holding her own with any policeman or chief constable in existence," observed the Vicar.

Finally the denouement, that wonderful moment in every case when Miss Marple revealed and reconstructed who it was who did it, how, and why. "That was really very simple," she would say, warming to her story, "but there wasn't any arsenic in the curry *then*," or "I noticed the palm in the pot by the window," or "it does remind me, just a little, of old Mrs. Trout." Thus she would proceed to unveil, before the dazzled eyes of her audience, an astounding array of clues, motives, village parallels, and facts never seen before in this particular combination—all adding up, to the dumbfounding of all, to the solution.

Appropriately, the most impressive finale of all her cases was played in the last one, *Nemesis*, before her most distinguished audience: an official from the Public Prosecuter's Office, the Assistant Commissioner of Scotland Yard, the Governor of Manstone Prison, and the Home Secretary. After listening to it all, the Home Secretary was asked his opinion of this elderly lady from St. Mary Mead. "The most frightening woman I ever met," he said.

So ended Miss Marple's career, and there can be no better way to end this biography of a most distinguished detective than with the words of Reverend Leonard Clement: "I had never liked Miss Marple better than at this moment."

A Miss Marple Bibliography

Marpelian bibliography is a discipline in itself. Listed here are most of the first appearances in print in the English language of the various editions of each title by Agatha Christie. Many of these editions have been reissued many times and are still in print.

The Adventures of the Christmas Pudding, and a Selection of Entrees (includes "Greenshaw's Folly"):
   London & Don Mills (Canada): Collins, 1960.
   London: Fontana, 1963. (PB)
   London: Collins, 1981.

Agatha Christie: Five Classic Murder Mysteries (includes *The Moving Finger*):
   New York: Avenel Books, 1985.

Agatha Christie's Detectives; Five Complete Novels (includes *The Murder at the Vicarage*):
   New York: Avenel Books, 1982

At Bertram's Hotel:
   London & Don Mills (Canada): Collins, 1965.
   New York: Dodd, Mead & Co., 1966.
   Roslyn, N.Y.: W.J. Black, 1966 (Detective Book Club).

New York: Pocket Books, 1967. (PB)
London: Fontana, 1968. (PB)
Leicester (UK): Ulverscroft Large Print Edition, 1968.
London: Collins, 1972 (Greenway edition).
New York: Dodd, Mead & Co., 1973 (Greenway edition).

See also omnibus volumes: *Miss Marple Meets Murder*, *A Miss Marple Quintet.*

The Body in the Library:
London: Collins, 1942.
New York & Toronto: Dodd, Mead & Co., 1942.
New York: Collier, 1942.
Roslyn, N.Y.: W.J. Black, 1942 (Detective Book Club).
Berne (Switzerland): Phoenix, 1943.
New York: Grosset & Dunlap, 1943.
New York: Pocket Books, 1946. (PB)
Harmondsworth (UK): Penguin, 1953. (PB)
London: Pan, 1961. (PB)
London: Fontana, 1962. (PB)
Leicester (UK): Ulverscroft Large Print Edition, 1972.
New York: Dodd, Mead & Co., 1985 (Winterbrook edition).

See also omnibus volumes: *Five Complete Miss Marple Novels*; *Murder in Our Midst*; *Starring Miss Marple.*

A Caribbean Mystery:
London & Don Mills (Canada): Collins, 1964.
Garden City, N.Y.: Doubleday, 1965 (Dollar Mystery Guild).
New York: Dodd, Mead & Co., 1965.
London: Fontana, 1966. (PB)
New York: Pocket Books, 1966. (PB)
Leicester (UK): Ulverscroft Large Print Edition, 1967.
London: Collins, 1978.
New York: Dodd, Mead & Co., 1979 (Greenway edition).

New York: Bantam Books, 1985 (Agatha Christie Mystery Collection).

See also omnibus volume: *Five Complete Miss Marple Novels*.

Double Sin, and Other Stories (includes "Greenshaw's Folly"; "Sanctuary"):
New York: Dodd, Mead & Co., 1961.
Roslyn, N.Y.: W.J. Black, 1961 (Detective Book Club).
New York: Pocket Books, 1962. (PB)
New York: Dell, 1964. (PB)
New York: Berkley Books, 1984. (PB)

Five Complete Miss Marple Novels (contains *The Mirror Crack'd; A Caribbean Mystery; Nemesis; What Mrs. McGillicuddy Saw!; The Body in the Library*):
New York: Avenel Books, 1980.
New York: Chatham River Press, 1984.

4.50 from Paddington:
London & Toronto: Collins, 1957.
London: Fontana, 1960. (PB)
Leicester (UK): Ulverscroft Large Print Edition, 1965.
London: Pan, 1974. (PB)
London: Collins, 1980.
New York: Dodd, Mead & Co., 1982 (Greenway edition).

Also published under the titles:
Murder She Said:
New York: Pocket Books, 1961. (PB)
What Mrs. McGillicuddy Saw!:
New York: Dodd, Mead & Co., 1957.
Garden City, N.Y.: Doubleday, 1958 (Dollar Mystery Guild).
New York: Pocket Books, 1958. (PB)
New York: Bantam Books, 1984 (Agatha Christie Mystery Collection).

A MISS MARPLE BIBLIOGRAPHY

See also omnibus volumes: *Five Complete Miss Marple Novels*; *Murder on Board*.

The Mirror Crack'd. See *The Mirror Crack'd from Side to Side*.

The Mirror Crack'd from Side to Side:
  London & Don Mills (Canada): Collins, 1962.
  London: Fontana, 1965. (PB)
  Leicester (UK): Ulverscroft Large Print Edition, 1966.
  Harmondsworth (UK): Penguin, 1974. (PB)
  London: Collins, 1980.
  New York: Dodd, Mead & Co., 1981 (Greenway edition).

Also published under the title:
The Mirror Crack'd:
  Garden City, N.Y.: Doubleday, 1963 (Dollar Mystery Guild).
  New York: Dodd, Mead & Co., 1963.
  New York: Pocket Books, 1964. (PB)
  New York: Bantam Books, 1984 (Agatha Christie Mystery Collection).

See also omnibus volumes: *Five Complete Miss Marple Novels*; *Miss Marple Meets Murder*; *A Miss Marple Quintet*.

Miss Marple: The Complete Short Stories (contains "The Tuesday Night Club"; "The Idol House of Astarte"; "Ingots of Gold"; "The Bloodstained Pavement"; "Motive v. Opportunity"; "The Thumbmark of St. Peter"; "The Blue Geranium"; "The Companion"; "The Four Suspects"; "A Christmas Tragedy"; "The Herb of Death"; "The Affair at the Bungalow"; "Death by Drowning"; "Miss Marple Tells a Story"; "Strange Jest"; "The Case of the Perfect Maid"; "The Case of the Caretaker"; "Tape-Measure Murder"; "Greenshaw's Folly"; "Sanctuary"):
  New York: Dodd, Mead & Co., 1985.

Miss Marple Meets Murder (contains *At Bertram's Hotel; The Mirror Crack'd; The Moving Finger; A Pocket Full of Rye*):
  Garden City, N.Y.: Doubleday, 1979 (Mystery Guild).

A Miss Marple Quintet (contains *The Murder at the Vicarage; The Mirror Crack'd from Side to Side; A Murder is Announced; A Pocket Full of Rye; At Bertram's Hotel*):
  London: Collins, 1978.

Miss Marple's Final Cases, and Two Other Stories (includes "Sanctuary"; "Strange Jest"; "Tape-Measure Murder"; "The Case of the Caretaker"; "The Case of the Perfect Maid"; "Miss Marple Tells a Story"):
  London: Collins, 1979.
  London: Fontana, 1980. (PB)

The Mousetrap, and Other Stories. See *Three Blind Mice, and Other Stories.*

The Moving Finger:
  New York & Toronto: Dodd, Mead & Co., 1942.
  New York: American Mercury, 1942.
  Berne (Switzerland): Phoenix, 1943.
  London: Collins, 1943.
  New York: Grosset & Dunlap, 1944.
  New York: Avon Book Co., 1948. (PB)
  London: Pan, 1951. (PB)
  London: Youth Book Club, 1951.
  Harmondsworth (UK): Penguin, 1953. (PB)
  London: Fontana, 1961. (PB)
  New York: Dell, 1964. (PB)
  London: Collins, 1968 (Greenway edition).
  New York: Dodd, Mead & Co., 1968 (Greenway edition).
  Leicester (UK): Ulverscroft Large Print Edition, 1970.
  New York: Bantam Books, 1983 (Agatha Christie Mystery Collection).
  New York: Berkley Books, 1984. (PB)

See also omnibus volumes: *Agatha Christie: Five Classic Murder Mysteries; Miss Marple Meets Murder; Murder in Our Midst.*

The Murder at the Vicarage:
  London: Collins, 1930.
  New York: Dodd, Mead & Co., 1930.
  New York: Grosset & Dunlap, 1932.
  Harmondsworth (UK): Penguin, 1948. (PB)
  New York: Dell, 1948. (PB)
  London: Fontana, 1961. (PB)
  London: Collins, 1976 (Greenway edition).
  New York: Dodd, Mead & Co., 1977 (Greenway edition).
  Leicester (UK): Ulverscroft Large Print Edition, 1980.
  New York: Bantam Books, 1983 (Agatha Christie Mystery Collection).
  New York: Berkley Books, 1984. (PB)
  New York: Bantam Books, 1985 (Collection of Mystery Classics).

See also omnibus volumes: *Agatha Christie's Detectives; A Miss Marple Quintet; Murder in Our Midst.*
Also published as a play:
Agatha Christie's Murder at the Vicarage, by Moie Charles and Barbara Toy. London: French, 1950.

Murder in Our Midst (contains *The Body in the Library; The Murder at the Vicarage; The Moving Finger*):
  Garden City, N.Y.: Doubleday, 1967 (Dollar Mystery Guild).
  New York: Dodd, Mead & Co., 1967.

A Murder Is Announced:
  London: Collins, 1950.
  New York: Dodd, Mead & Co., 1950.
  Roslyn, N.Y.: W.J. Black, 1950 (Detective Book Club).
  New York: Pocket Books, 1951. (PB)
  London: Fontana, 1953. (PB)
  London: Pan, 1958. (PB)

  Leicester (UK): Ulverscroft Large Print Edition, 1965.
  London: Collins, 1967 (Greenway edition).
  New York: Dodd, Mead & Co., 1967 (Greenway edition).
  New York: Dodd, Mead & Co., 1985 (Winterbrook edition).
See also omnibus volumes: *A Miss Marple Quintet; Murder Preferred; Starring Miss Marple.*
Also published as a play:
A Murder Is Announced, by L. Darbon. London: French, 1978.

Murder on Board (includes *What Mrs. McGillicuddy Saw!*):
  New York: Dodd, Mead & Co., 1974.

Murder Preferred (includes *A Murder Is Announced*):
  New York & Toronto: Dodd, Mead & Co., 1960.

Murder She Said. See *4.50 from Paddington.*

Murder with Mirrors. See *They Do It With Mirrors.*

Nemesis:
  London: Collins, 1971.
  New York: Dodd, Mead & Co., 1971.
  Roslyn, N.Y.: W.J. Black, 1971 (Detective Book Club).
  New York: Pocket Books, 1973. (PB)
  London: Fontana, 1974. (PB)
  Leicester (UK): Ulverscroft Large Print Edition, 1976.
  New York: Bantam Books, 1984 (Agatha Christie Mystery Collection).
See also omnibus volume: *Five Complete Miss Marple Novels.*

The Nursery Rhyme Murders (includes *A Pocket Full of Rye*):
  New York: Dodd, Mead & Co., 1970.

A Pocket Full of Rye:
  London & Sydney: Collins, 1953.
  New York & Toronto: Dodd, Mead & Co., 1953.

Garden City, N.Y.: Doubleday, 1954 (Dollar Mystery Guild).
New York: Pocket Books, 1955. (PB)
London: Fontana, 1958. (PB)
Leicester (UK): Ulverscroft Large Print Edition, 1963.
New York: Dodd, Mead & Co., 1981 (Greenway edition).

See also omnibus volumes: *Miss Marple Meets Murder; A Miss Marple Quintet; The Nursery Rhyme Murders.*

The Regatta Mystery, and Other Stories (includes "Miss Marple Tells a Story"):
New York: Dodd, Mead & Co., 1939.
New York: L.E. Spivak, 1939 (abridged edition).
New York: Grosset & Dunlap, 1940.
New York: Avon Book Co., 1946. (PB)
New York: Dell, 1964. (PB)
New York: Berkley Books, 1984. (PB)

Sleeping Murder:
London: Collins, 1976.
New York: Dodd, Mead & Co., 1976.
New York: Bantam, 1977. (PB)
London: Fontana, 1977. (PB)
Leicester (UK): Ulverscroft Large Print Edition, 1978.
New York: Bantam Books, 1985 (Agatha Christie Mystery Collection).

Starring Miss Marple (contains *A Murder Is Announced; The Body in the Library; Murder with Mirrors*):
New York: Book of the Month Club, 1977.
New York: Dodd, Mead & Co., 1977.

Surprise! Surprise! A Collection of Mystery Stories with Unexpected Endings, ed. by Raymond T. Bond (includes "Greenshaw's Folly"; "The Case of the Perfect Maid"):
New York: Dodd, Mead & Co., 1965.
New York: Dell, 1966. (PB)

They Do It With Mirrors:
London: Collins, 1952.
London: Fontana, 1955. (PB)
Leicester (UK): Ulverscroft Large Print Edition, 1966.
London: Collins, 1969 (Greenway edition).
New York: Dodd, Mead & Co., 1970 (Greenway edition).
London: Pan, 1971. (PB)
London: Fontana, 1975 (new edition). (PB)

Also published under the title: *Murder with Mirrors:*
Garden City, N.Y.: Doubleday, 1952 (Dollar Mystery Guild).
New York: Dodd, Mead & Co., 1952.
New York: Pocket Books, 1954. (PB)
New York: Bantam Books, 1985 (Agatha Christie Mystery Collection).

See also omnibus volume: *Starring Miss Marple.*

13 Clues for Miss Marple, a Collection of Mystery Stories (contains "Tape-Measure Murder"; "Strange Jest"; "Sanctuary"; "Greenshaw's Folly"; "The Case of the Perfect Maid"; The Case of the Caretaker"; "The Blue Geranium"; "The Companion"; "The Four Suspects"; "Motive v. Opportunity"; "The Thumbmark of St. Peter"; "The Bloodstained Pavement"; "The Herb of Death"):
New York: Dodd, Mead & Co., 1966.
New York: Dell, 1967. (PB)
New York: Dell, 1975 (new edition). (PB)

13 for Luck! A Selection of Mystery Stories for Young Readers (includes "The Blue Geranium"; "The Four Suspects"; "Tape-Measure Murder"):
New York & Toronto: Dodd, Mead & Co., 1961.
New York: Dell, 1965. (PB)
London: Collins, 1966.

The Thirteen Problems (contains "The Tuesday Night Club";

"The Idol House of Astarte"; "Ingots of Gold"; "The Blood-stained Pavement"; "Motive v. Opportunity"; "The Thumbmark of St. Peter"; "The Blue Geranium"; "The Companion"; "The Four Suspects"; "A Christmas Tragedy"; "The Herb of Death"; "The Affair at the Bungalow"; "Death by Drowning"):

London: Collins, 1932.
London: Pan, 1961. (PB)
London: Fontana, 1965. (PB)
Leicester (UK): Ulverscroft Large Print Edition, 1968.
London: Collins, 1972 (Greenway edition).
New York: Dodd, Mead & Co., 1973 (Greenway edition).

Also published under the titles:
Miss Marple and the Thirteen Problems:
Harmondsworth (UK): Penguin, 1953. (PB)
The Tuesday Club Murders:
New York: Dodd, Mead & Co., 1933.
New York: Grosset & Dunlap, 1934.
New York: Avon Book Co., 1958. (PB)
New York: Dell, 1963. (PB)
New York: Berkley Books, 1984. (PB)

Three Blind Mice, and Other Stories (includes "Tape-Measure Murder"; "Strange Jest"; "The Case of the Perfect Maid"; "The Case of the Caretaker"):
New York: Dodd, Mead & Co., 1950.
New York: Dell, 1980. (PB)
New York: Berkley Books, 1984. (PB)
New York: Dodd, Mead & Co., 1985 (Winterbrook edition).

Also published under the title:
The Mousetrap, and Other Stories:
New York: Dell, 1952. (PB)

The Tuesday Club Murders. See *The Thirteen Problems.*

What Mrs. McGillicuddy Saw! See *4.50 from Paddington.*

A List of Miss Marple Short Stories and the Editions In Which They Appeared

Listed here are the Miss Marple short stories as they appear in the Christie bibliography. A number of these stories have been anthologized elsewhere, occasionally under different titles.

"The Affair at the Bungalow"

in: *Miss Marple: The Complete Short Stories*
The Thirteen Problems
The Tuesday Club Murders

"The Bloodstained Pavement"

in: *Miss Marple: The Complete Short Stories*
13 Clues for Miss Marple
The Thirteen Problems
The Tuesday Club Murders

A List of Miss Marple Short Stories

A List of Miss Marple Short Stories

A List of Miss Marple Short Stories

Also published under the titles: "The Case of the Retired Jeweller"; "A Village Murder."

"The Thumbmark of St. Peter"   in: *Miss Marple: The Complete Short Stories*
The Thirteen Problems
The Tuesday Club Murders

"The Tuesday Night Club"   in: *Miss Marple: The Complete Short Stories*
The Thirteen Problems
The Tuesday Club Murders

"A Village Murder." See "Tape-Measure Murder."

Miss Marple Feature Films

1962   *Murder She Said* (MGM), with Margaret Rutherford as Miss Marple; adapted from *What Mrs. McGillicuddy Saw! / 4.50 from Paddington.*

1963   *Murder at the Gallop* (MGM), with Margaret Rutherford as Miss Marple; adapted from the Hercule Poirot novels *Funerals Are Fatal / After the Funeral.*

1964   *Murder Ahoy* (production and screenplay by MGM), with Margaret Rutherford as Miss Marple.

1964   *Murder Most Foul* (MGM), with Margaret Rutherford as Miss Marple; adapted from the Hercule Poirot novel *Mrs. McGinty's Dead.*

1981   *The Mirror Crack'd* (EMI), with Angela Lansbury as Miss Marple; adapted from *The Mirror Crack'd / The Mirror Crack'd from Side to Side.*

Miss Marple TV Movies

1956   *A Murder is Announced* (NBC, Goodyear Television Playhouse), with Gracie Fields as Miss Marple.

1984   *A Caribbean Mystery* (CBS Television), with Helen Hayes as Miss Marple; adapted from *A Caribbean Mystery.*

1985   *Murder with Mirrors* (CBS), with Helen Hayes as Miss Marple; adapted from *Murder with Mirrors / They Do It with Mirrors*.

1985   *The Body in the Library, A Murder is Announced, The Moving Finger, A Pocket Full of Rye* (BBC), with Joan Hickson as Miss Marple.

References

Auden, W.H. "The Guilty Vicarage." *Harper's*, (May 1948).

Christie, Agatha. *An Autobiography*. New York: Dodd, Mead & Co., 1977.

Christie, Agatha. *Cards on the Table*. Greenway edition. New York: Dodd, Mead & Co., 1968.

Christie, Agatha. *Curtain*. New York: Dodd, Mead & Co., 1975.

Christie, Agatha. "The Market Basing Mystery." (English title: *Poirot's Early Cases*) In *Hercule Poirot's Early Cases*. New York: Dodd, Mead & Co., 1974.

Christie, Agatha. *The Murder of Roger Ackroyd*. Greenway edition. New York: Dodd, Mead & Co., 1967.

Christie, Agatha. *The Mystery of the Blue Train*. Greenway edition. New York: Dodd, Mead & Co., 1973.

Christie, Agatha. *Poirot Loses a Client*. (English title: *Dumb Witness*.) New York: Dell, 1965.

Lathen, Emma. "Cornwallis's Revenge." In *Agatha Christie, First Lady of Crime*, ed. by H.R.F. Keating. New York: Holt, Rinehart and Winston, 1977.

Ramsey, G.C. *Agatha Christie, Mistress of Mystery*. New York: Dodd, Mead & Co., 1967.

AGATHA CHRISTIE

Mystery's #1 Bestseller!

"One of the most imaginative and fertile plot creators of all time!"
—Ellery Queen

Agatha Christie is the world's most brilliant and most famous mystery writer, as well as one of the greatest storytellers of all time. And now, Berkley presents a mystery lover's paradise—35 classics from this unsurpassed Queen of Mystery.

"Agatha Christie...what more could a mystery addict desire?"
—The New York Times

_____09317-4 CARDS ON THE TABLE
_____08900-2 THE PATRIOTIC MURDERS
_____09324-7 MURDER IN MESOPOTAMIA
_____09180-5 MURDER IN THREE ACTS
_____06803-X THERE IS A TIDE...
_____09855-9 THE BOOMERANG CLUE
_____06804-8 THEY CAME TO BAGHDAD
_____08770-0 MR. PARKER PYNE, DETECTIVE
_____09483-9 THE MYSTERIOUS MR. QUIN
_____06781-5 DOUBLE SIN AND OTHER STORIES
_____06808-0 THE UNDERDOG AND OTHER STORIES
_____08796-4 THE MOVING FINGER
_____09853-2 SAD CYPRESS
_____09854-0 POIROT LOSES A CLIENT
_____09362-X THE BIG FOUR
_____09152-X DEATH IN THE AIR
_____06784-X THE HOLLOW
_____09845-1 N OR M?
_____06802-1 THE SECRET OF CHIMNEYS
_____09482-0 THE REGATTA MYSTERY AND OTHER STORIES
_____09318-2 PARTNERS IN CRIME
_____06806-4 THREE BLIND MICE AND OTHER STORIES
_____06785-8 THE LABORS OF HERCULES

All titles are $2.95

181/b